OUTLET

RANDY TAGUCHI

TRANSLATED BY GLYNNE WALLEY

VERTICAL.

Copyright © 2003 by Randy Taguchi

All rights reserved.

Published by Vertical, Inc., New York.

Originally published in Japanese as *Konsento* by Gentosha, Tokyo, 2000.

ISBN 1-932234-04-7

Manufactured in the United States of America

First American Edition

Vertical, Inc.
257 Park Avenue South, 8th Floor
New York, NY 10010

1

It was an unpleasant awakening.

The air conditioning must have been turned up too high. My throat was parched and I felt nauseated.

Slipping out from between the sheets, careful not to wake the guy sleeping next to me, I took a bottle of mineral water from the fridge and downed it in one gulp. I felt sluggish. I'd drunk too much. My body was still struggling to process the alcohol.

I fished my glasses and my laptop out of the carryall I used for work. After connecting the adapter, I crawled around the floor of the hotel room until I finally found a free outlet behind the TV, and plugged the adapter in. Moving around distracted my system enough that I no longer felt like puking. I turned over the phone beside the bed and connected its cord to my laptop's modem. I pushed the power button. The computer came on, its motor humming faintly.

I liked this moment. A light kindles on the screen, the hard drive clicks restlessly as it gets to work. It was like life was being breathed into it.

"Move it, move it, my little elves."

I was sitting on the floor leaning forward and tapping the

keyboard when the guy called out to me.

"What're you doing?"

For some reason, I felt embarrassed, as if I'd been caught red-handed at something.

"Oh, nothing."

When I looked back, the guy, still naked, was raising himself up drowsily to look at me.

"Internet?"

"Mm-hmm. I wanted to see how the market was doing."

The guy put his middle finger to his eye and began to rub it. He was probably as hung-over as I was.

"Work?" he asked.

"Yeah, something like that."

I wished he'd just go back to sleep. I didn't want to be interrupted.

"I don't get stocks. Is it fun?"

I get that question a lot. Are stocks fun? Of course they are. The stock market is the mechanism behind everything. I'm mystified by people who can go on living without knowing that.

"It's weird more than anything else," I answered. "Men drive the market, but it behaves like a hysterical woman. It has violent ups and downs; it goes off at the slightest provocation. But it also has great intuition—it can tell the future, and sometimes brings about synchronicity—on a global scale. The economy is kind of occult."

I gazed at the figures lined up endlessly on the screen. At first glance it's just a meaningless series of numbers, but when you watch the market daily you're sometimes struck by certain sequences. Like when you see a peaceful, beautiful lawn and notice that one corner of it has been mowed in a different direction. It's fun to discover those patches. I lay on my belly on the floor staring at the computer screen, and the naked guy behind me didn't know what to do with himself.

"Hey…" he mumbled.

"What?"

"This wasn't a one-night stand, okay?"

I lifted my head and looked at him. He was still sitting up, gazing at me far too seriously. He looked sad, and a little lost. With his head cocked at a forty-five degree angle, and his bare shoulders sloping gently, he looked just like Dustin Hoffman acting his heart out.

I snorted, trying to stifle a laugh, and said, "Knock it off."

In the end, I went back to sleep again at around dawn. It was almost noon by the time I got back to my apartment.

He'd left at eight that morning, saying he had to shoot some photos—all the while acting so considerate it was annoying. I waved without getting out of bed. As soon as I was alone I got really drowsy, and slept soundly until the wake-up call from the front desk.

I left the hotel. Steamy heat was rising from the asphalt. Right, August began today. It was hot. The city in summer had a tropical fruit scent.

As I walked toward the station the lower half of my body felt raw and exposed, as if the muggy air were seeping into it.

After serious sex I always feel like I've forgotten to put on my underwear: I feel terribly naked and defenseless under my skirt.

He'd entered me again toward dawn, as if to confirm something.

It took him a long time to come, maybe because he was hung-over. He banged his waist against me greedily. He was far more violent and dominating than he had been the night before. I clung to him and accepted it all. His desire crawled up inside me. If I allowed it, I could resonate with a man and come any number of times.

But no matter how many times I climaxed, he wouldn't finish. He kept slowly working my quivering vagina. As I synchronized my breathing with his, new waves of pleasure came over me.

"You're like a different person when you're being made love to," he told me. Maybe so. When my desire's spent I lose all interest in men.

It was already after noon when I got back to my condo in Kichijoji.

I'd worked up a sweat just walking around Shibuya. I wanted to soak in a lukewarm bath and get the alcohol out of my system. I filled the tub. The sound of rushing water began filling up my head, and it frightened me. Like I might flow out with it.

Why did I sleep with Kimura? There were gaps in my memory of the night. We were doing a story on a new on-line securities firm—he was the photographer—and after we'd visited the company we had dinner together. I'd invited him. Then we went barhopping, got shellacked, and went to a "love hotel" in Maruyama-cho.

Whoosh. Water running. Thoughts were overflowing, I couldn't get them straight. I sat there staring vacantly at the water rising in the tub when the phone rang.

I snapped out of my daze and hurried to answer it. The words were slammed into my head with particular high-handedness.

"Taka's dead."

It was Dad's voice.

For a second, the floor turned flimsy soft and began to sink under my weight.

"When?" I asked.

"No idea," Dad spat out. "He rotted down to a slime, no one can tell," he muttered. "Just come home. Got it? Don't dawdle. It's getting crazy here." On that thoroughly scolding note he hung up.

I put down the receiver and sank into a chair. The flood kept gushing forth from my head. *Whoosh.* I felt nothing. Just awfully transparent.

My older brother was dead.

My breath still smelled of booze and my temples throbbed. Blood vessels contracting and convulsing.

Anyway, my brother was dead and I had to go home.

I took the dry-cleaner's cover off my funeral clothes and started to pack. I faxed my office, put on my makeup, shut the door tightly and slowly turned the key. When I stepped outside I was in for a shock. It was already evening. I could smell grilled fish from the pubs in front of the station. Kids home on summer vacation walked around in little groups. The world was a pleasant soft glow of twilight unconcerned with death. My sense of time was off. I felt dizzy. It was as if I had stumbled into a monochrome world.

My brother had gone missing about two months before.

I found myself accepting his death with extreme calm. I'd had a feeling it would end this way.

Maybe my brother had been hovering up near the love hotel ceiling the night before, watching me have sex. He'd died and come to bid a last farewell, only to find his sister plastered and getting fucked. Glancing up past the guy's shoulders my eyes might have met my brother's expressionless gaze. I shuddered. Maybe it was to avoid that kind of thing that I always kept my eyes shut during sex.

2

It was eight in the evening when I arrived at the little station in the mountains near the Kofu Valley.

The lightless mountains surrounded the town in black.

I'd intended to take a cab, but there wasn't one to be found. So I crossed the deserted rotary and set out on the twenty-minute walk home.

There was a rundown supermarket across from the station. It used to be pretty popular, but ever since a brand-new shopping center had opened up on the other side of the station, the old shopping street had begun to fall apart. Once, when I was a kid, there was a fire at the supermarket. Sparks flew, torching up the night. My brother and I and some people from the neighborhood gathered to watch the darkness glow.

I walked down the street that ran along the tracks, past the supermarket, and the road gradually grew narrower. The town petered out and was replaced by rice paddies. It used to be a farm road, but now it was nicely paved, with streetlights glowing along the way.

It was just a little strip of paddies between hills, but the smell of summer grass was almost noxious. I quickened my pace, waving away little moths that flew into my face.

I used to ride my bike home from school on this road, after club meetings. It came back to me now, vividly. The rasp of my bike's unlubricated front wheel, the bumps and potholes on the dirt path communicating themselves to my pubic bone.

Who was I? Was I the same person who'd been in a Shibuya love hotel just that morning? The hired hand of a financial magazine who worried about deadlines, who'd just faxed her office? Real life was fading like a dream. Memories of the past lived again, revived by the smell of thick vegetation. The *me* who had once lived here, once walked this road, was awakening. The humid midsummer darkness clung to my skin. Countless insects were twirping. Living things, concealed, breathing in the night. Nothing had changed.

My brother, too, had taken this road to go to school.

It was when he was in junior high. Playing in the paddies, I could see him coming home from school. He was ten years older than me, so I was probably about six at the time. He always walked hunched over, eyes narrowed, as if angry. My brother as I remember him then was already living in another world.

Come to think of it, I didn't have many childhood memories of my brother. I could recall fragments and incidents, but I couldn't remember the things you did together every day. Was he even at the dinner table? He must have been, but I couldn't picture him there.

What I remembered was him picking on me.

He picked on me a lot when I was little. He'd come home from school and say, "Hey, Yuki, let's play pro wrestling." Then he'd pin me with a headlock or a cobra twist. I'd cry and scream from pain, but he wouldn't quit. Once he even dislocated my hip.

It always started out as fun. Somewhere along the line it would turn real. That happened a lot. Suddenly a switch somewhere inside him would flip and he couldn't hold himself back, his demeanor would change. One minute he would be smiling; the next, stone silent. He'd beat me with a blank stare. Eyes wide open, pupils unfocussed. Not looking at me, not looking at anything. He'd go on punching me, driven by something terrifying. I thought, at such times, that he might kill me.

Beyond the lit stretch of the paddy road, something white moved.

I froze in fear.

As I gingerly peered into the darkness, a white dog appeared out of the tall grass.

Hey, it's Shiro, I thought. Shiro (which means "white") was the dog my brother had kept for just a brief time when I was a kid. She was a stray, and a smart one. My brother had picked her up somewhere and let her live under the porch. He'd squeeze his allowance to buy her fish sausages. He really loved her.

No way, I thought. Shiro was dead.

One day my dad came home trashed and beat her to

death.

Shiro was in heat, and she and this brown mutt were mating. Dad saw them and lost control. He grabbed my brother's baseball bat and started walloping them. It was midafternoon, on a Sunday. Dad had been holed up in some friend's house in the neighborhood drinking since the night before, and was absolutely out of his skull.

Still connected to the mutt, Shiro hobbled around, yelping, until Dad let her have it one more time. Hearing her cries, my brother ran out of the house, but when Shiro saw him she just growled and tried to get away from him too. She tried to edge back, abject with fear. She collapsed and breathed her last.

So the dog couldn't be Shiro.

That had all been more than twenty years ago. The dog shot a glance in my direction, then trotted noiselessly down the paddy road. I followed the dog.

Up ahead was an unmanned railroad crossing.

A lot of accidents happened there; some people called it the "man-eating crossing." Crossing there and turning left brought you to a path that followed the river. There it was even darker, but it was a shortcut to my house.

A girl killed herself at this crossing.

She didn't go to my school. I only knew her by sight. Just an average girl, with freckles scattered across her face. That morning we were leaving on our class trip. The girl had waited for the train jammed full of high-school girls and thrown herself in front of it. Rumor had it that one of ours had stolen her boyfriend; she had gotten back at us. Maybe.

Ever since then, everyone was afraid her ghost would appear at that crossing. Her body had been torn apart, and one of her arms was never recovered. People in town said a stray dog had probably found and eaten it. The story was that she still wandered looking for her lost arm.

The red light was flashing at the unmanned crossing.

The thunder of an approaching train came through the rails, disturbing the air. Shiro turned to look at me, then barked once and ran across.

I moved to chase after her, but at that instant the warning bell began clanging and pulled me back.

I could see somebody in the darkness on the other side of the crossing come swiftly up to Shiro. The figure appeared out of nowhere. Shiro wagged her tail gleefully.

"Taka?" I yelled. "Taka, is that you?"

My voice got lost in the clanging of the bell and didn't seem to reach them. The figure didn't turn to look at me. But from behind it looked like my brother, thin and stooped. I thought of crossing, but the blood-soaked ghost of that girl flickered in my mind's eye. I was afraid the man-eating crossing was sucking me in.

"Taka!" I yelled again, and the figure slowly turned to look.

Just then I heard a roar, and the blur of a train rushed past between us. My eyes had adjusted to the dark and the light from inside the cars was blindingly bright.

When the train disappeared from view, Shiro and my brother were gone.

"Hey, I saw Taka at the railroad crossing," I said as I took my shoes off in the entryway at home. My dad came out and grabbed me by the collar.

"Stop talking stupid."

His breath already smelled of alcohol.

"He's dead. Dead! I saw him with my own eyes. He was rotting, melting away. His face...I couldn't bear to look at it. It was awful. There were maggots crawling out of his eyeballs. It was the most pathetic thing I've ever seen!"

Dad began crying bitterly in spite of himself.

"Where's his body?" I asked Mom.

"At the hospital," she answered, through tears.

"What was the cause of death? Suicide?"

She shook her head.

"It wasn't suicide? So why...?"

She was tongue-tied, and she looked at Dad. He was kneeling in the hallway with his head down, choking back sobs. As I stood in the gloomy entrance to my home, smothered in uncomfortable silence, I remembered. *That's right, these people never say the important things.*

3

The first person to find the body was a woman from the realtor's office.

My brother had gone to them looking for an apartment in early June. According to them, he looked scruffy but he dealt with them politely and properly. He said he'd like to see a two-room apartment which got a lot of sun, and as soon as he saw the place he signed the lease. He paid the first two months' rent up front. But thereafter no payment ever came. The agent in charge of the property got suspicious and sent a woman from the office to call on my brother.

Standing at the door, she said, she'd smelled something odd.

She said it stank of rotten fish. She wondered if an animal had died in the apartment or something. My brother hadn't even put a nameplate on the door yet. There were no signs that anybody lived there. She wondered if he'd ever moved in.

She used the master key to unlock the door.

The minute the door opened, a horrific stench rushed out of the room.

Reflexively she covered her mouth with her hand, but she couldn't prevent herself from vomiting. She began to suspect that something awful had happened. The door opened onto a small entryway that connected to the kitchen. She peered inside and saw a man lying on the plastic tile floor. Blackish-red blood had congealed on the tiles. Waves of nausea washed over her, and she shut the door and threw up until she could taste bile. Then, sobbing, she ran back to the office.

The realtor called the police, the police called Dad, and Dad called me, at three in the afternoon on the first of August.

An autopsy determined that my brother had died from heart failure. The police explained to my parents that he'd probably wasted away in his apartment in the midsummer heat.

The day after I got home, Dad took me to see Taka's apartment.

He'd been drinking since morning. He couldn't drive in that condition, so we took the train, getting off at a dreary station on the Chuo Line.

It was terribly hot. Under the scorching sun we stopped at a convenience store to buy flowers, and Coca-Cola, which my brother had loved.

Dad walked ahead of me in silence. He was always talking in his head to somebody. If he was silent it was because he was deep in conversation with his other self. Sometimes he clicked his tongue or muttered "goddamnit." When something unpleasant happened, Dad always got mired in vicious circles of thought. His mind played them over endlessly. At times like that, it was as though he couldn't even see me.

We left the shopping street and entered a quiet residential neighborhood. After we'd walked a little way, we encountered an odd smell.

It can't be. We turned at a corner where there was a small shrine to Inari, the fox deity, and the odor grew worse. It smelled like rotten fish. We came to a brand-new apartment building and we could tell that the tenants were opening their windows and doors slightly to peek out at us. All of them were covering their mouths with handkerchiefs or towels.

"This is it," Dad said, indicating an apartment on the first floor by the street.

It smelled so bad that just standing in front of the room I wanted to puke. I was shocked. *Does it always stink this bad when someone dies?*

We opened the door. The corpse had already been carried away, but a copious amount of blackish blood had congealed into a jelly on the kitchen floor and maggots were crawling around in it.

The stench of human decomposition resembled that of rotting tuna.

I was overwhelmed by the sight of the pool of blood, which outlined the shape of a human being. It bore the definite trace of my brother's form.

Normal responses to the sight and smell went out the window. I knelt in front of the pool of blood in that stuffy kitchen in the middle of summer and pulled the tab on the Coke he'd loved so much.

I was sure it would have been his last wish. He was

addicted to Coca-Cola—he drank it like water. So much that it had started to eat away his teeth. I set the can of Coke and the convenience-store flowers down by the pool of blood and briefly brought my palms together.

"What a stench. How is it that it doesn't bother you?" Dad had covered his nose and mouth with a hand towel, and was trying to yank the window open.

"Hey, you can't open that. It already smells bad enough in the neighborhood."

"But it stinks. I can't stand it."

Finally, he said he'd wait for me outside.

Alone, I looked around the dismal room. What the hell had happened to my brother here? I wanted some sort of clue.

The first thing that caught my eye, there in that room where Taka had died, was a vacuum cleaner.

It was leaning against a pillar in the small living room. It was still plugged into the outlet, looking for all the world as if someone were just about to start cleaning.

Next to the vacuum sat a brand-new plastic bucket. Inside it were a bottle of MagiKleen household cleanser, a bathroom sponge, and a cleaning rag. In the bathroom was a toilet cover still in its plastic wrapper. A bottle of Mama Lemon detergent had been placed by the sink. In the bath was a scrub brush and a plastic bath-bowl, both with the price tags still on.

The objects continued to exist, unaltered.

Only my brother, the organic body, had gone and

changed.

My brother had rented this place himself.

It was pretty far from the station, but it got a lot of sun. Maybe that's what had attracted him. Then one day he came over to clean the place prior to moving in. He'd bought cleaning supplies at the nearby convenience store, opened the sliding doors, put together the vacuum, and plugged it into the outlet. Then, just as he was thinking of getting down to work, something had happened to him and he'd given up on cleaning.

Now that he was dead, of course, there was no way of knowing what had happened, why he'd quit.

He'd carefully leaned the vacuum, still plugged into the outlet, up against the post. Then...then what? Probably lied down.

Perhaps he'd lain there vacantly gazing out the window until the sun had set.

When night came, and it was dark, he'd lit the lone light bulb he'd screwed in.

Then he'd taken the curtains he'd bought to cover the windows, spread them out on the tatami mats instead of a futon, and lain down again. Maybe he'd stayed like that until morning, or maybe he'd gotten hungry and gone out shopping, or maybe he'd drifted off to sleep. In any case, it seemed as if my brother had spent several days like that, doing nothing.

As though he'd been inspired to just quit living.

In July in a hot, humid room, my brother abandoned the business of living.

He'd soon gone through what little money he had. Even then, he didn't pack up and leave. After a while, possibly worried about people looking in from outside, he'd shut the sliding door, despite the raging heat. In the steamy room he'd continued his desultory existence.

It seemed that at night he'd leave the room and walk over to the convenience store to buy cup o' noodles and comics. There was a stack of weekly comics a couple of feet high next to the curtains he'd been using as a bed. From the dates on them it seemed that he'd gone out up until about three weeks ago.

Soon his money was gone. He stopped going out altogether. What in the world did he do alone in the dark room?

The only things he'd brought over to the apartment with him were about thirty CDs. There was a Walkman next to his pillow. He'd been listening to Mozart last, which was odd. Taka had been into jazz.

He'd probably wasted away quickly from the heat and hunger. But why did he have to stay shut up in this room, sweltering, starving?

In the closet were a few items of clothing and a change purse. Just a few shirts and some underwear, wadded up in a gym bag. Why had he brought a change of clothes? Had he really intended to set up house like this in this unfurnished apartment?

My brother had lived at home with our parents for the

previous few years. He didn't have any furniture or household goods of his own. In which case, had it been his intention to come here to lie down and wait for death?

The change purse was in the gym bag. There were thirteen yen inside. It wouldn't buy a measly piece of candy.

This probably represented my brother's entire fortune when he died. He didn't have a job. He'd withdrawn completely from human society for five years. Just how had he intended to live when he'd taken this apartment? Why had he moved here? It didn't seem like a place just to die in. It was a cute little apartment, more appropriate for newlyweds.

The curtains my brother had been using as a bed still retained wrinkles in the outline of his body. A plastic shopping bag from the convenience store served as a trash can. A look inside revealed half-digested noodles vomited into tissues. He'd probably been so weakened by the heat that he couldn't keep anything down.

An alarm clock he'd brought kept ticking away the time, even after his death.

When I looked at it closely, I realized the clock was mine. It was a small, square, gold-plated number. I'd gotten it from the local Lions Club for winning a composition contest in junior high school. The gold plating had mostly peeled off. That was ages ago—fifteen years. He'd probably found it at my parents' house and taken it.

I picked it up. The clock had come to me when I was fifteen, witnessed my brother's death, and was returning to me now, when I was almost thirty. The little clock had kept on marking the time just so it could see Taka die.

I packed up Taka's sparse belongings and slipped the clock into my own bag. As I did so, I wondered if matter had memory. Was my brother's state of mind at death's door somehow recorded by this clock?

When we got back home there was an undertaker waiting for us.

He was a slightly stout man, fiftyish, wearing a black suit and black-rimmed glasses. Mom fixed me with a pleading look as I got home. She was a wreck, incapable of any decision or action whatsoever. She just held a handkerchief to her nose, crying her heart out.

Undertakers force bereaved families to make tedious practical decisions. He spoke without expression:

I understand your feelings, but in any case, there has to be a funeral. And it must be held soon. This is because your brother's body is badly compromised, in fact it is in an advanced state of decomposition. It's the middle of summer. There's a limit to how long and well he can be preserved with dry ice. He needs to be cremated before he rots any more.

When my mother heard this she began wailing like a madwoman.

The undertaker pushed us through all the groundwork necessary for this major event. *What religion should the service be? What's your budget for the funeral? How many mourners will be in attendance? Where will they be coming from? Where will they stay?* His pushiness felt good. It's his business, I realized. He was used to it. Families probably wouldn't be able to decide anything if they didn't have an undertaker coaxing things along.

"You have three options for lunch at the crematorium: regular, deluxe, and super-deluxe."

"What's the difference between regular and deluxe?" I asked.

He looked at me and grinned. "Deluxe includes deep-fried shrimp."

He continued: "Next, considerations for mourners bringing funeral offerings. There's the three-thousand-yen package, the five-thousand-yen package, and the ten-thousand-yen package...."

We decided one thing after another, gradually returning to reality. Yes, reality—the survivors have to go on living in it. I was reminded of that. An undertaker is someone to be grateful for. When your world has been shaken, maybe getting bogged down in mundane real-world details is a form of escape. Regardless of who's alive and who's dead, the deluxe lunch comes with deep-fried shrimp and the regular doesn't, and that's the way it is.

A true veteran of funerals, the undertaker chose his words with great care.

His condolences were truly touching, and he did nothing to aggravate the bereaved family's state of mind more than he needed to. He was businesslike in the best sense of the word. His professional instincts seemed to have told him that the only person in the house capable right then of making sensible judgments was the headstrong daughter. So all the preparations for the funeral ended up being made between the two of us.

I spent the time between the wake and the funeral bound to the undertaker in curious camaraderie.

Those were an oddly restful couple of days. It was a relief not to be with my parents. Being with the undertaker was far more comfortable than being with Mom and Dad.

That's what it means to be a pro, I found myself thinking again and again. Owing to the special condition of my brother's corpse, the funeral ended up costing quite a bit. But I was grateful to the undertaker, and didn't begrudge him a bit of his fee. Me, who up until then had thought there was no bigger waste of time and money than a funeral.

"Listen, I want to see my brother's body." I took the undertaker aside before the wake and made my request.

"Miss, I don't think that's a good idea," the undertaker said. "The body has already started to decompose. It's hardly recognizable."

"I want to see him anyway. I have to see what kind of condition he was in."

The man replied, "I've been in this business for thirty years, so believe me when I tell you it's not a good idea. I wouldn't mislead you. You don't want to look."

"Why? You people saw him. Why can't I?"

"Because I'm a stranger. To a stranger a corpse is just an object, but you're a relative. You'll likely end up regretting it.

Don't."

"What sort of reason is that? Why would I regret it just because I'm a relative? I'll be all right. I just want to see my brother one last time."

"That's just not a good idea. You'll have to welcome back his spirit every summer during the Lantern Festival. You'll think about him every year. Don't you think you ought to remember him as he was, looking good?"

I still wasn't convinced, but the undertaker was firm and wouldn't let me open the coffin lid. I peered in through the little window. The body was wrapped in blue industrial plastic and buried in dry ice.

I saw that being an undertaker was no simple task.

We held my brother's funeral in the ceremonial hall of the funeral parlor. The first floor of the building, believe it or not, was used for weddings; funerals were held upstairs. It struck me that joyous occasions and tragic ones really weren't all that different. There's only a thin line between them.

The undertaker stuck around for the wake, too, all night long.

Sometime in the middle of the night I offered him a glass of sake. "Thank you very much," he said, and drank it down respectfully. I began to feel a certain affection for the man. Maybe I really was shaken up after all—maybe I was lonely.

"Okay, here's the deal," I started out. "On my way back to my parents' after hearing the news about my brother, I saw him on a farm road. He was standing on the other side of an unmanned railroad crossing.... Do you think that's strange?"

He was kneeling formally, and for a while he remained silent, thinking. Then he looked up and answered, "No. I don't think that's strange." He sounded sincere enough.

"Someone like you, with your job, do you—have you ever had mysterious experiences like that? Seeing ghosts, that kind of thing?"

The undertaker looked me full in the face and answered, serious as ever, "No. I've never seen a ghost. I've been in this business for thirty years, but I've never once seen anything like that. If they exist, I wouldn't mind laying my eyes on one, but unfortunately, no."

"Hmm...Yeah, I guess it was just a hallucination."

For a while, the undertaker didn't respond. He just sat there like an *objet d'art*. Then finally, he opened his mouth. "Everybody dies. Every day, somebody dies somewhere. Death is nothing rare for undertakers. It's our business. If people don't die, we're in trouble. And because it's business for us, we can't afford special feelings for the dead. We make them pretty so that their families will have an easy time saying farewell, we treat them with care just like when they were alive, and we take them to the crematorium. That's all."

He paused long enough to swallow and take a breath. "The only thing I find mysterious is that people seem to follow each other in death. It's an odd thing. Speaking from experience, I can tell you that funerals tend to cluster in places. In fact, just today there were two other funerals in villages near your house. Funerals tend to gather like that, like wrinkles in fabric. I don't know why, but the dead summon the dying."

I had weird thoughts listening to the undertaker.

The night before last, before hearing the news about Taka, why had I slept with Kimura? We'd been friends for years, and I'd never felt romantic toward him. In spite of that, I suddenly wanted him. Was my brother calling to me? The sex act seems awfully close to death. Maybe my lust came from a premonition of my brother's death. Ah, but that couldn't be it. He'd already been dead for three weeks when they found him.

"There are those who say they've been visited by dead relatives in dreams," the undertaker continued in a monotone, knocking back the second glass of sake I offered him. For some reason, the guy never seemed to blink.

"In dreams?"

He nodded silently. "That's right. I don't remember when it was, but once we were holding a wake in this very room. In the middle of the night one of the bereaved calls me over and says that someone's knocking at the sliding-glass door at the entrance to the building. But I can't hear a thing. He gets angry. 'What are you talking about? Someone's banging at the glass door. Can't you hear it?' I can't, but I suggest we go take a look. We go downstairs to the entrance."

I gulped.

"The shutter is closed. And of course, I don't hear a thing, but the man says, 'He's knocking! It has to be my dead father. Open the shutter!' So I open the shutter—what else could I do? Of course, there's nobody there. But the man rushes outside, and he kneels down and is saying farewell to someone. I'm just watching quietly from behind. This person talks for a long time, gets more and more emotional, and finally collapses on the ground. When I come closer I see that he's fast asleep. I realize then that some waking dream was to blame. He must have been pretty tired. The next day, he doesn't even remember telling me to open the shutter. You see, at funerals everybody's upset. They only remember half of what they do anyway. So I have to be very thorough about everything, at every step of the way, or else it causes problems later."

"You didn't tell the man anything?"

The undertaker shook his head like a wind-up doll. "I don't remind the bereaved of things they've forgotten. If they forget something, it means they don't need to remember it. Being with the bereaved like this day in and day out, I've come to realize that they do ten times the number of things they actually remember doing. But they forget, because there's no need to remember."

It made sense.

Although I didn't have many memories of my brother, I'd spent years with him. That was a fact. But I'd almost forgotten about it. Probably because I didn't need to remember—there was just no reason to. Taka's time and mine had always been out of sync. Strangely, they seemed to be converging now that he was dead. His time and my time were somehow falling into step.

From the moment of death, a person becomes a speechless thing. A speechless thing is like a mirror. Every time I thought about my brother, I was looking at myself: my past, my life.

I had to recover those lost memories then.

The next day was the funeral. In the morning, a priest came to read sutras.

"That superior gives good sutra," the undertaker whispered.

"Is that right?"

"Yes. You got lucky, getting him."

"What's 'good sutra'?"

"Reciting them with heart, I guess you could say. Listen to them for enough years and you can start to tell the difference."

"You mean he reads them well?" I pressed the point.

The undertaker's poker face was motionless for a good while before his lips parted again. "They used to say the singer Hibari Misora was a genius. But can you put in plain words the difference between a good singer and a bad one? When you hear them, though, you can tell right away. It's kind of like that."

That made sense. And, sure enough, the sutra reading that day made Mom and Dad cry.

It had been hot since early morning. The weather report warned of a typical midsummer day with temperatures well into the nineties. The undertaker kept mopping his brow as he checked on the dry ice in the coffin.

"This heat is going to melt the ice pretty quick. You can

already smell it. This won't do. You'd better light more incense, a lot more. You know, that's why people started burning incense at funerals, to hide the smell of the body."

I did as he said and began lighting more and more incense, but the higher the sun rose the more the body reeked. My brother was decomposing some more.... The undertaker brought some especially strong-smelling incense, and we lit all of it. The funeral parlor filled with so much smoke you would have thought the place was on fire.

"I used to think that when someone dies, it's the end, but I guess you keep changing afterwards too," I commented.

The undertaker nodded. "That's right."

"You know, my brother's rotting and reeking makes me feel weirdly close to him. I'm already used to the unpleasant smell, and it tells me that he still exists. When the smell's gone, I'm sure I'll forget about him before long. I'm always like that. I only think about myself. My brother often used to tell me I was arrogant. It's as if by rotting like this, he's hollering, 'Hey, I'm here, I existed.' That's how I feel. He's telling me, 'I really was alive, get it?' I feel like he's speaking to me. Is that strange?"

The undertaker grinned and said, "Not a bit."

As they filed through the billowing smoke, the mourners pressed handkerchiefs to their noses. Some of them even gagged as they lit their incense. Everyone was covered with oily sweat.

After my brother had fully overwhelmed the mourners with his stench and imposed his presence on them, his body was taken to the crematorium. Too bad we couldn't let him keep rotting to the very end.

I didn't know if that was his wish, but since he'd chosen to live as a sloth, I wanted him to consummate his lifestyle in death. Instead he was incinerated in a furnace, transformed suddenly into odorless ash while I ate my deluxe lunch.

4

It was hot enough to make you dizzy. The cicadas' screeching sounded like death throes.

I just couldn't be inside, so I waited in front of the apartment, under the blazing sun. I was waiting for the cleaners.

The undertaker had put me in touch with "a company that specializes in cleaning and disinfecting rooms which have had corpses lying in them."

Other companies wouldn't accept jobs like that, cleaning rooms that stink of death.

They were supposed to arrive at eleven. The truck pulled up two minutes late.

Out from it stepped a tall, slender guy about my age. He wore a blue jumpsuit. I figured he was just a part-timer and that his boss was stepping out next. But the good-looking young man handed me his business card and told me he was "in charge." And it's neither flattery nor exaggeration when I say he was handsome. Incredibly. With his deep eyes he looked like a young Indian bonze. His manner was polite, his speech was pleasant, and he had a sense of humor. He seemed like he knew what the world was about and what in it there was for him to do.

The first thing he did was offer me his condolences.

His words weren't the same social niceties I'd heard from so many people already. They had real tenderness, as if he really understood how I felt. There was something about him that reminded me of the undertaker. I realized that here was another professional who'd dealt with lots of situations like these. People who made a living out of other people's deaths had to get the knack for condolences.

I showed him into the apartment. When I opened the door to the kitchen we saw the layer of congealed blood covering the plastic tiles; maggots crawled in the cake. Right away he asked, "Is this the only blood?"

"Yeah."

"So, this blood is the source of the odor. If we remove these tiles and incinerate them, the smell should disappear in about a week. That's good. Your brother was really considerate."

I almost burst out laughing. Considerate? My brother Taka, who'd only ever made his family suffer?

"What makes you say that?"

"Well, he died on the tiles, and not on the tatami mats. If he'd died on the mats, given the season, the maggots would have gotten down into the mats themselves, and the room would be unrentable. But, as is, once we replace all the tiles and disinfect the place, it can be rented out in three months."

Was that how it was? Despite the platitude about "wanting to die on a tatami mat," doing so could be a pain in the neck for the bereaved.

"Why did he bleed so much, if he wasted away?" I muttered, half to myself.

"When dead people are left lying around, they start leaking blood from every orifice. It doesn't have to be a grisly accident—just leave a body and it'll start bleeding."

At this point the landlord came by on a bicycle.

As soon as he saw my face, he said, "Are you the family?" and started complaining. *Because of this people are going to think the apartment's creepy and nobody's going to rent it. Ugly rumors are going around. The two-year-old kid next door can't eat anymore because of the smell. The parents say they're going to move out before their kid starves to death. The people on the second floor are moving out, too. And they say it's because Apt. #1 made life impossible for them. They want me to pay their moving expenses. Take responsibility and shoulder the expenses.* He went on and on railing at me about things like that, showering me with spit.

He just kept talking, and neither I nor the young man could get a word in edgewise. We just looked at each other. The landlord had obviously rehearsed this conversation in his head several times on his way over. He'd already anticipated all of my responses. People who rehearse things in their head like that tend to let their thoughts guide them in the worst possible direction.

The neighbors across the street were watching the scene through open windows, covering their mouths with towels.

It was awfully hot, and there was no air conditioning in the apartment. My head was swimming. I didn't know where to begin, so I just stared, blankly, at the tufts of hair poking out of the landlord's ears.

"You know, you were actually pretty lucky," the guy from the cleaning company suddenly retorted. "The smell will be completely gone from this room in a week. The resident died on the tiles. This kept the damage down to a bare minimum. I've seen a lot—I mean a *lot*—of rooms where people died. If the body had been left lying on a tatami mat for a week or more in the middle of summer, we wouldn't be standing here talking like this. The smell of a body rotting on tatami mats is so bad that it makes our new hires quit the same day. Detectives new on the job end up vomiting at the scene and getting chewed out by their superiors. That's how bad it is. I'd need a mask to do my job. The mats get soaked through with blood and become a nest of maggots. Flies' eggs would line the screen door. Sometimes, if the room is on the second floor, the mats get so heavy from the blood that the ceiling on the first floor begins to sag. In cases like that, it's not just the apartment but the whole building that's kaput. But this place came out all right. He died on the tiles, so he did minimal damage. You're a lucky man. In three months this apartment will be rentable. I don't see cases like this too often."

The landlord looked as if he wanted to say something, but kept quiet.

"If it'd satisfy the neighbors, how about if I arranged for all the apartments to be deodorized?" I asked the landlord, but the cleaner shook his head.

"That won't be necessary. If I just disinfect this room, the smell will go away just fine. All we have to do then is leave the door and windows open to let the air circulate. There's no reason for you to waste money like that."

He said he'd be back the next day to remove the tiles and disinfect the place.

The landlord asserted himself one more time, grumbling, "That'd better take care of the smell." Then he left.

"So how do you get rid of the odor?" I asked, as the landlord rode away.

My throat was parched. I took out the cans of oolong tea I'd brought along, and offered one to the cleaner. Together we gulped down some tea, watching maggots swim in a sea of slimy blood.

"The smell comes from particles. It's not so much that we get rid of the smell, it's more like we overwhelm the smelly particles with particles of a different scent. And then we just wait for the smelly ones to go away. Pretty soon they'll be undetectable to the human nose. It's the same principle as your regular deodorizers. I believe it's the same with incense at a funeral: people started burning incense during the wake because the body would be rotting. Of course, these days they have chemicals that slow down the decomposition process significantly. But in the old days, when they still buried people, they used incense to hide the stench—incense is a strong odor-killer. In fact, why don't we light some today before we leave?"

So we stuck some incense sticks in our empty tea cans and

lit the sticks.

Then we each pressed our palms together in prayer.

How many times had I already brought my hands together since my brother's death? Not that I had any idea what to pray for. What was prayer anyway? Every time I pressed my palms together and bowed I was at a loss. What did it mean, appeasing the dead? What were other people thinking when they did this? What were they asking for? What did they feel during these moments?

I stole a glance at the young man next to me. He had his eyes closed and his palms pressed together tightly. I thought his prayer pose was just beautiful. He was obviously used to it, but I had no clue what he was thinking or feeling.

He said suddenly, "You know, the body doesn't really die."

"Huh?"

"The human body goes on as an entity, it just keeps changing. If you leave it alone, it goes stiff, the blood runs out, it rots, maggots appear—it keeps going through stages. Microorganisms break it down and it returns to nature. An abandoned corpse keeps living and changing. Ever since I began doing this I've become really interested in death. Does this kind of talk gross you out?" He glanced at me, worried.

"Not at all."

"Good. I feel like your brother died a very mysterious death. Call it a hunch, based on experience." He looked around the room.

"You think so?" I asked. "It really bothers me, too, to tell you the truth. I mean, it's strange, isn't it? Just look at this place. What was he doing here? Everything's halfway. Nothing's finished, nothing's complete. It's like...like one day his batteries just ran out. Here, look at this. The vacuum cleaner's still plugged into the outlet. What do you make of that?"

He appeared stuck for a moment, then offered, "Maybe he was about to start cleaning?" He checked the vacuum's dust-bag. "See, it's got a fresh dustbag on it. He was going to vacuum."

I stared at the insides of the dustbag. "If he was about to start cleaning, why did he just stop? You said you've seen a lot of rooms that had dead bodies in them. Is it true that some people leave messages when they die? I don't mean people scrawling their murderers' names as they die, like on TV, but something more...unconscious. Don't they say that when people die they subconsciously communicate their thoughts to somebody? Do you know what I mean?"

He thought for a while before answering. "I do. Sometimes when I clean a place, I find myself going, 'Oh, so that's what he was thinking.'"

I waited for him to continue.

"I don't remember exactly how long ago, but we went once to clean up after an old man who'd died in bed. As we were disinfecting the place, we noticed something odd about the ceiling. Small, round stickers. I thought, what in the world? What's with all the stickers? There were more than I could count, stuck all over the ceiling. Well, it turned out they were fluorescent—after you turned out the light, they'd glow for a while, like stars. The old guy had been making his own Milky Way there on the ceiling. When we pulled the curtains, turned the light on, and turned it back off, there it was, a beautiful rendition of the Milky Way. It was kind of surprising. The apartment was in a public housing complex in Kasai, and there was nothing around it but concrete—highways and all. Really impersonal. But it turned out the man was from an island way down south near Okinawa—Amami. As he died he was probably thinking about the gorgeous night sky he could see back home."

Without thinking, I looked at the ceiling. Of course there was nothing there.

"You know, my brother starved to death in this room. He was only forty, and he was healthy. But he just shut himself up in this room lying around doing nothing, getting gradually weaker from the heat and hunger, until his heart gave out and he died. I don't understand. He rented the apartment, and he plugged the vacuum cleaner into the outlet like he was going to start cleaning the place. But he gave up, not only on cleaning, but on living."

The young man folded his arms and walked toward the tatami room which still had my brother's things. "It doesn't seem to me that your brother meant to give up on life. If he had, I think he would have died in the tatami room, which he was using as a bedroom. He died on the tile floor in the kitchen. I imagine he went there because it was just a little cooler, which means he was thinking up until the end. Plus, he died in a place that's nearer the outside than the bedroom.

Only three steps from the front door. He chose a spot where he could crawl outside if he needed to. It looks to me as if he still wanted some connection with the outside world. I don't think he really wanted to die."

"Then, why did he?"

"Could he have come in here for some water and died of a heart attack?"

I shook my head. "They say he was cradling his head on his arm, using it as a pillow. He didn't look at all like someone who'd collapsed in agony."

I carefully unplugged the vacuum cleaner.

"This might be my brother's message to me. Before he died he used to tell me something about outlets."

The young man took out a pair of pliers and snipped off the cord near the end and gave me the plug. "We'll take care of the other items, as you requested."

Thin wires stuck out where he'd cut the cord. The plug sat there in my palm like a shriveled-up bird's foot.

5

Five days' worth of newspapers were jammed in my mail slot.

They'd been wedged in and were hard to pull out. As I wrestled with them I could feel the delivery boy's annoyance. His animosity seeped out from the bundle of papers.

Oh, no. I can't let myself tune into that kind of thing.

I shook my head and tried to screen out the malice emanating from the crumpled papers. I get totally exhausted when anyone's hatred gets through to me. My brother's funeral had tired me out and weakened my defenses.

My apartment was stuffy from being sealed for five days. I hadn't taken out the kitchen garbage before leaving, and now it was giving off a foul odor.

It was hot. I turned the air conditioner on "high" and stuck my head in the fridge.

There was a message from Kimura on the answering machine.

No matter how intense, sex never stayed in my memory long. My tryst with Kimura felt like something that had happened ten years ago.

"*Beep*. It's Kimura. Uh, I heard the news at the office. I

don't really know what to say. You must be going through hell right now. Don't let it get to you. Seems like all I can say is mundane shit like that. Sorry. Cheer up, be strong. Give me a call when things settle down. Bye."

The minute the funeral ended, I knew I had reached my limit emotionally.

Dad kept blaming Mom. My brother had died like that "because you didn't raise him right."

You spoiled him. That's why the sonofabitch never turned into a man. You spoiled him when I wasn't around, and look what a mess he turned into. Dying like that. I can't even look people in the eye. You failed me....

Most likely, Dad felt that it was really he who'd killed my brother. Mom felt guilty too. And so did I, maybe. Everyone in the family was feeling personally responsible for his death, and Dad, the weakest, couldn't take it and was blaming Mom.

Mom usually showed some resilience in the face of Dad's verbal abuse, but this time she just didn't have it in her. She took to bed. Dad was usually worse to her when I was around. Mom was weakening, Dad was drunk and disorderly, and I couldn't watch him torment her anymore.

I really don't like my family much. Both Dad and Mom go off at the slightest thing, crying and wailing, but the next thing you know they're laughing, forgiving each other, making up—and then they're at it again. Their place is always a vortex of intense emotions. Rays of unfocussed destructive feelings irradiate me when I'm with them. Every time I come home from their place I collapse in utter exhaustion.

I felt haggard from the heat, the smell, and the lack of sleep.

I wanted to meet someone normal. Anyone. Just somebody quiet and unemotional. Somebody who'd comfort me like I was a child, who'd say, *That was awful, that was hard, you handled it really well.*

Kimura's voice on the answering machine was calm and kind. I realized I was dying to see him.

"What a shock. He died the very next day, right? The day after...you know." Kimura had brought beer, and he pulled the tab on one as he spoke. "You don't want one, Yuki?"

I shook my head and took a bottle of zubrovka from the freezer.

"What's that?"

"Zubrovka. Want some?"

"You keep alcohol in the freezer?"

"It doesn't freeze. It just gets a bit thick." I poured some into a glass with some ice. He asked what exactly it was. Medicine, I answered. I like zubrovka precisely for its mouthwash-like taste and smell.

"I hate alcohol fermented with yeast. It tastes too raw, too fresh."

Kimura looked puzzled as he muttered, "Weird." Then, "Must have been tough."

I nodded, sitting down beside him. He'd seated himself on the edge of my bed as if it were a sofa.

He said, "You know, you really surprised me…last time."

"Why?"

"Why? I mean, first you got sloppy drunk, and then you said you wanted to have sex."

"I did?"

"Yeah. Don't you remember?"

"Nope."

"You hailed a cab, and then you yelled at the driver to take us to the nearest love hotel, it didn't matter which one."

"I don't remember that part at all." I was lying. I remembered it all.

"Oh. So you don't remember, huh?"

Kimura was visibly saddened. He'd been fond of me for a long time. I'd known that. I called him up only when it was convenient for me; he was just someone to kill time with. I was totally confident that I'd never sleep with *him*. I couldn't understand my own actions that night, inviting him to a love hotel. Was it that I'd had a premonition of my brother's death? For some time now, perhaps, I'd been in bad shape mentally and emotionally.

"Well, anyway, I was glad you called," he said. He proceeded to place his lips on mine, and the smell of beer assaulted me. Without meaning to, I pushed him away.

He looked at me, obviously hurt by the unexpected rebuff. "What's wrong?" he asked.

I felt nauseated and put my hand over my mouth. "I remembered something unpleasant." The smell.

When he'd brought his lips close to my face the reek of

death in my brother's apartment had come back to me. Particles of that smell were entering my nostrils. It was weak and faint, but there was no mistaking it: the smell of death.

"Are you all right? You look pale." Kimura looked so panicked it was pitiful.

Feeling sorry for him, I curled up against his chest. "I'm all right now. Sorry."

I could hear him breathing above my head. And once again, particles of that scent infiltrated my nostrils, burrowing deep inside. No mistake. It was Taka's death-stench. But why was it coming from Kimura?

I looked him in the face. "Hey, did you eat anything strange before coming over?"

"No. Why?"

"I smell something."

"What?"

"I'm not sure…"

I was at a loss. I couldn't tell him he smelled like death. Instead I sniffed at his shirt and his socks like a dog.

"Hey, hey, what's going on? Do I stink that bad?"

"It's not that."

"What's not what? Stop it," he said, and started sniffing at himself.

As seriously as I could I said, "Hey, breathe in my face, will you?"

"What the hell? Does that turn you on?"

"Just do it. Hurry."

Reluctantly, Kimura exhaled in my face. Just as I'd

thought, I could just barely detect a few particles of that rotten-tuna smell. It was hardly an odor, so subtle it was more of a feeling. But my nose was just sensitive enough to sniff out the particles from among many others. The smell of blood and flesh rotting in the summer heat. An organic, rancid smell, maybe even a little sweet.

"Actually, my breath is on the fresh side, don't you think?" Kimura was trying to sound cheerful.

"Hey, anything wrong with you, health-wise?"

"No. What—"

"Nothing at all?"

"Nothing at all. I'm in perfectly good health."

"Well, if you start feeling a little sick, go see a doctor, okay?"

"What are you talking about?" He fixed me with a serious look, but I couldn't very well tell him that he stank of death. "Are you trying to tell me I smell sick?"

As I watched Kimura sniffing himself, I began to wonder if the problem wasn't with him but with me. "No. I guess I'm just a little freaked out because of the way my brother died. I had to take care of cleaning up the apartment he'd died in and everything. It's just my nerves. All kinds of smells are bothering me all of a sudden. It's me, not you. Sorry."

Kimura gave me one of those compassionate looks he was so good at. "I understand." He squeezed my hand. "Your brother's dead. You have every right to feel on edge right now. It's perfectly natural."

This time he didn't try to hug me. He seemed to be holding himself back. I'd said something to him I shouldn't have. But it was definitely *that* smell. And there was no way I could bring my mouth into contact with a mouth that gave off that smell.

Kimura left, telling me to be sure and rest. I saw him to the door. As he was tying his shoelaces he let out a small, beery belch. And there it was again, the faint scent of death.

There must be something wrong with me, I thought. Still, I got a can of deodorizer from the bathroom and sprayed the doorway with it. Even then, I could pick up the smell; it was there among the particles of spray. Police dogs had nothing on my nose. Shit.

In medical terms, this had to be a case of obsessive-compulsive disorder.

Obsession with a particular smell. They diagnosed that sort of thing. I sprawled out face-down on bed, my head in my hands. When I closed my eyes I became even more sensitive to the smell, but I kept them shut so I could try to remember. I tried to remember the guy from the cleaning company, and the undertaker. I wanted to see them again. It was a peculiar longing, yet I thought, *On a night like this, how comforting it would be if they were with me.*

The cleaning guy had arrived right on time for the second appointment.

He used a big cutter to peel off the blood-encrusted tiles. He chopped them into yet smaller pieces and then stowed them away in a black plastic bag. It was another hot day. The neighbors covered their mouths with handkerchiefs and quickened their pace as they walked past.

I visited them with gift certificates for beer. "I apologize for all the trouble we've caused you. I can assure you that what happened wasn't any kind of *incident*, so please don't be alarmed. The smell should be gone by the end of the week. I'm truly very sorry." I did this because the head of the block association had come by to let me know that I "really ought to pay my respects to the neighborhood."

Without a doubt, the smell of death made people uneasy. It made them feel like they'd touched a corpse.

"It's so bad we can't even eat," said the housewife next door, a hand-towel tied over her mouth.

But the young man from the cleaners kept on working without a mask. He stuffed the plastic bag into his truck, then took off his gloves and disinfected his hands. After that he walked over to me.

"It's all right now," he said, briskly. "I've eliminated the source of the smell. Now, if we just let the outside air in, the odor should disappear."

He went back inside the apartment and walked around spraying, eventually emptying a whole can of deodorizer into the rooms. "That was an air-freshener spray just like you'd buy in any store."

I watched him work. It was sad to think that when this was over he'd disappear from my life forever. I asked him, "How did you get into this business? Did you get hired straight out of school?"

Without interrupting his spraying, he gave a bashful smile and answered, "Yep, right out of school. Actually I joined without really checking to see what they did. I was pretty surprised at first, let me tell you. I thought about quitting, many times, but somehow I just couldn't. I'm not quite sure why not. It's a job nobody wants to do, but I guess it fascinates me. On this job I learned just how many ways there are of dying. I always knew there were many ways to live, but I hadn't realized the same was true of death. I guess I'd had a vague notion that most people probably breathe their last in a hospital. But that's just not true. They die in a lot of different ways. An infinite number of ways—most people don't know that. And gradually I came to be really drawn to the way people die. My job is to carefully cover up the tracks of the departed, to erase the shadow of death from people's houses. But I can't help feeling that it's also a way of laying the dead to rest."

"Laying to rest?"

"That's right. Maybe it's presumptuous, but I want to give their souls rest. I don't know why, but doing this makes me feel good. That's all there is to it."

"And you never thought it was gross?"

"At first I did, but I'm used to it now. People are surprisingly good at adapting, you know. I guess we can get used to anything."

Now I wanted to see him again and ask him what was happening to my sense of smell. Working with smells was part of his job, so he might be able to tell me. Was my nose oversensitized due to shock? Or was the smell just an illusion? Was it a temporary thing? Or would I have to go on like this?

I lay face up on the bed for a while, letting my thoughts drift. I found myself recalling that unmanned railroad crossing. The figure I'd seen on the other side—that had definitely been Taka. No mistake about that. I'd never for a moment believed in ghosts. I'd never seen one. Nevertheless, I was sure it had been my brother.

Maybe it was just as Kimura had said. Maybe I'd been more deeply traumatized by my brother's death than I'd realized.

6

The dank hallway leading to the lab was empty. Not a soul in sight. The aging university building was as dark and cheerless as ever. Supposedly the Old Campus was slated for demolition next year. I figured fate had brought me to it one last time before it disappeared.

I thought I'd never come back. But I couldn't think of anyone else to turn to. With each passing day it became clearer that something abnormal had happened to my sense of smell.

In fact, I'd encountered that smell again in the crowded train on the way. Among the mingled odors of sweat, deodorant, hair-care products, B.O., and insect repellent, my nose picked out particles of that ol' rotting-corpse smell.

Where was it coming from?

I felt a little nostalgic every time I smelled it. I'd think, *Hey, that smells like my brother rotting.* When I focused on the odor, I could even follow—only vaguely, of course—the path of the particles. The source wasn't far away, I could tell. Weaving between passengers, I sought the source. The smell seemed to be coming from a lone strap-hanging salaryman, from his navy-blue suit.

Why was such a smell on his suit?

It was, though, and unmistakably. I sidled up next to him to make sure. Particles of the odor clung to the fabric of his suit as if it had been stored next to a dead body. The salaryman looked calm as he clenched the strap and stared out the window. He looked to be about forty, a totally run-of-the-mill guy. Neatly dressed. Aside from the fact that he was cloaked in that death-stench, there wasn't anything remotely out of the ordinary about him.

I stole a glance at his face, and our eyes met. He had single-edged eyelids that looked like they'd been cut out with a blade. Terrified, I moved away from the man.

The particles continued to waft leisurely across the car. I could almost see them.

When I got off the train at the station where the university was, the summery fragrance of the grass and trees lining the sidewalk comforted me.

How many years had it been since I'd last come here? The campus was known city-wide for its greenery. The moment I was on it I could feel the temperature drop several degrees. I felt that old familiar coolness in the air, a coolness peculiar to college campuses. In the old days I'd walked around as if I'd owned the place. Now there was only one person here who would know me—the man I'd come to see.

From somewhere I heard the disharmonious jumble of a practicing brass band. It was still summer vacation, so there weren't many people around. I walked through the arched entrance to the building and down the dim hallways. I was seized with the odd sensation that I was walking back through time. I thought, *The heart is always ready to return to the past.* The past is always there inside us. People are nothing but concentrates of memory.

I came to a stop in front of a shabby old sign that read *Psychological and Psychiatric Research Laboratory*. A melancholy sigh escaped my lips. I was still not sure about seeing Atsuo Kunisada again.

I was worried the meeting would turn unpleasant. He might get vindictive. It had always been easy for Kunisada to hurt me with words. Maybe if I pretended I still liked him we could work things out peacefully. But I doubted I could do that.

I knocked, and heard him say, "Come in," in that high, nasal voice of his. I took a deep breath and opened the old wooden door. Kunisada's lab was as moldy as it had been ten years ago. It still smelled of mildewy paper and bad breath.

"Well, well, well. What have we here? I haven't seen *you* in a long time."

He swiveled in his armchair a hundred and eighty degrees and offered me a dramatic greeting. Ten years, and the same mannerisms.

"Professor. Nice to see you again." I bowed politely. I looked up again to find him fixing his former protégée with an appraising look.

He said, "I never thought you'd be the one to initiate contact again. You surprise me."

"Yes, well...I've been remiss. How are you?"

"Just fine, of course."

His words rang hollow; they concealed little barbs.

"I know you're busy, Professor, and I'm sorry to take up your valuable time. The thing is, I have a problem, and I want your opinion."

"Of course, I'll help in whatever way I can. You were a special student, Yuki."

It gave me gooseflesh to hear him pronounce my name in that ominous way of his. He was just as unctuous as he'd been ten years ago.

Once, Kunisada had been my lover.

Back then I was majoring in psychology, and Kunisada was my advisor. It was a rule that students training to become professional counselors had to undergo counseling as part of the major—it was called "educational analysis." And I received mine from him. Once a week, for about four years, I made a record of my dreams, and with them as my guide I'd wandered the world that was my head.

Often, during the course of analysis, the patient starts to feel romantic towards the therapist. In clinical terms, it's known as transference. I was tripped up by it and I fell deeply in love with Kunisada.

In most cases, the patient is able to work through the transference on the way to recovery. In fact, transference isn't looked upon as particularly problematic, but rather as a necessary evil arising naturally from the treatment. Of course, that's assuming the counselor behaves sensibly and refuses to indulge the patient's infatuation.

But every once in a while, a therapist doesn't manage to completely stave off a client's advances, and instead begins to harbor romantic feelings of his or her own in return. It's known as countertransference. Sometimes the situation culminates in a physical relationship.

Over the course of my "educational analysis," Kunisada and I had become entangled in a web of transference and countertransference. Before they knew it, teacher and pupil were stuck in a morass of passion.

For the first two years, I'd kept telling myself, *This is just transference. It's nothing more than a temporary infatuation*. But my feelings for Kunisada kept growing and growing, until by the beginning of my junior year my desire to own him had trounced all reason. I couldn't suppress it. If I couldn't be accepted and loved by the man, then life had no meaning for me anymore. So I confessed my love to him. That is to say, I came on to him. Aggressively.

"This is nothing. You're simply experiencing transference. I presume even you realize that much?" At first Kunisada tried to admonish me—but I was already sensing an erotic response from him. I stood on the edge of the abyss of desire and tried to entice him in. And he played along, pretending to be simply overwhelmed by his student's youthful passion.

"What is it about me that stimulates you? Analyze your impulses for me." He'd often pose this kind of question to me. And like a faithful lackey, I praised him. I could tell that I was whetting the appetite of a voracious ego. After that, what we did ceased to be therapy. It was a domination game. I wanted to say whatever he wanted to hear, anything that would please him. I'd let him dominate me as much as he wanted. I allowed myself to fall prey to his desires. Because letting oneself be dominated is the same thing as dominating.

After our counseling sessions we'd go out to dinner, then go for a drive in his car. He'd park in an empty lot near the harbor. At that point, he'd always say, in his theatrical fashion, "We simply cannot go on doing this." Which was the signal for me to start weeping and pleading with him as I took his penis into my mouth. For hours on end, there in the car, Kunisada would lick my nipples and play with my genitals. But we never had sex. "I won't put it in, you know," he'd say. "It's my policy never to cross that line with my students."

And after this had gone on for about a year, when our lust had reached its absolute highest pitch, we had intercourse.

Kunisada was a sadist, so from the start he had me tied up. Maybe that was why he'd spent a year simply toying with my body—maybe he got pleasure out of making me writhe. I wanted it so bad I was afraid I'd go crazy—all I wanted was for him to take me. So I did whatever he told me.

He had the ropes ready. He tied me up on the bed. He bound me carefully in a weird position, with my hands and feet tied together behind my back, so that my genitals were lewdly exposed. He slowly, gently stimulated them, splayed open like that as they were. The way he did it was meticulous and not at all forceful; he drove me to numbing heights of pleasure. I believe I was being broken in.

Kunisada dominated me completely, mind and body. And I found unsurpassed pleasure in being dominated by him. I wondered if I truly was a masochist. I'd never dreamed there was such happiness in thinking nothing and letting things be done to me.

But about a year into our relationship, I began to get tired, both of being dominated by Kunisada and of sex with him in particular. My transference was wearing off. Kunisada was an ideal man who listened attentively to everything I had to say—during analysis. As soon as the session was over he became sadistic, selfish, arrogant, infantile. I'd finally started to notice what he was really like.

Once I had my eyes open again, he was no more than a self-conscious, childish man. It shocked me how suddenly I lost interest in him. Suddenly his very touch made my skin crawl. Every puerile ploy he used to keep me from leaving, every over-emphasized word he spoke nauseated me. And in the end, I ditched him, the man I'd once respected and adored. I did it coldly, contemptuously.

But there was no way he could forget the way I'd squirmed and squealed when he was doing it to me, the way I'd so gladly slobbered on his penis. He would remember that forever, and overlay the sight of the real me with his memory of the way I had been then. I couldn't face his gaze, so I avoided seeing him altogether.

Even now, I could tell that was how he was looking at me. He was remembering: what my genitals tasted like, the way I would move my hips like a madwoman when I was just about to come. And he was appraising me, trying to fathom whether or not the flame still burned in me. Fully confident that it did.

"Here, have a seat. I regret that I've no coffee to offer you. Are you thirsty?"

"I'm okay."

I sat where he indicated I should.

"It must be something fairly serious, if it's brought you here to see me."

I avoided his gaze as I tried to think of where to begin.

"It's about my brother…"

"Your brother?" He opened his eyes wide and brought his palms together in front of his chest. His usual pose.

"He died last week."

"Is that so? Oh, my. You have my condolences. This would be the brother that…"

"I think I mentioned him to you a few times. You may remember."

"Yes, well, only the general outlines. I always try to forget everything about old clients. Let me see, your brother had some emotional problems, didn't he? You said you thought he was a borderline case, am I right?"

"Yes. But I was never able to decide if he was sane or mentally ill." He had problems, but I didn't know if that made him outright crazy. Things might have been better if he'd been clearly insane.

"Did your brother…commit suicide?"

I shook my head. "I don't even know if it was suicide or not. He just stopped living, almost carelessly. He starved to death. I just don't understand why he'd do such a thing. Was he sick? Was he in his right mind? Did he kill himself? Or did he die without meaning to? That's why I came here—I'd like to get your objective assessment."

Kunisada heaved a sigh. "Hmm. Well. Let's talk about your brother a little. Start anywhere you'd like."

Being accepted like that was a relief to me—even if that acceptance was nothing more than an attitude cultivated by long professional training. Against my will, I flashed back to the moment I'd fallen in love with him. Ten years ago, he'd been the only man in the world who'd ever tried to understand me. I had clung to him with all my soul, all my power.

What had been bothering me then, anyway? I couldn't remember. The analysis had failed. My heart had been freeze-dried and stashed away in my subconscious.

"I...don't have much in the way of memories of my brother. He was ten years older than me. I have clear memories from about the age of four, but he isn't part of them. He only starts to appear from when I'm about six, and even then, all I have are fragments. When he died—that was when I first noticed that I don't have many memories of him. When he left home at eighteen after graduating from high school, I was eight years old, just a third-grader. I remember that pretty well. We were going to have a graduation party for him and he'd invited some friends from school to come over. Mom cooked something special, which she hardly ever did, and Dad splurged on beer for the occasion. And then we waited for his friends to show up. We waited late into the night, and nobody came. The situation got more and more awkward, and my brother got more and more depressed. He was pretty quiet usually, but that night he talked a lot. Which felt unnatural— we could tell he was really upset. That was maybe the only time I felt sorry for him. See, I hated my brother. He started picking on me when he was in junior high. That was also when he started to get violent toward Mom. I think my brother must have been pretty difficult in junior high. He calmed down some once he started high school. But still, he could never really control hismelf—his emotions blew up in his face a lot. He was a real music freak in high school, and evidently he desperately wanted his own stereo system. When Mom refused he just went crazy, threw a tantrum. He wouldn't speak for days, and at every opportunity he'd take his frustration and anger out on Mom. She finally gave in and got him what he wanted. She said she was afraid he'd be the death of her otherwise. I remember being disturbed by the whole thing, as young as I was. How was he going to make it through life like that, unable to control himself?"

"What do you think now, objectively? Do you think he was mentally ill?"

"No, I think he was emotionally unstable in junior high and high school, but other than that I think he was a normal teenager. He had problems with self-control and with interpersonal communication, but I think he was otherwise a normal teenager."

But even as I said it, I wondered just what "normal" was. Just where did I draw the line? I didn't know.

"After high school, for some reason my brother went to work for a company in Nagoya. I remember him cursing and yelling at Mom as he left the house. He railed at Mom and Dad for being ignorant. We lived in Kofu, and my brother was the only one from his class in high school to go to work in Nagoya. I had no idea why he chose to go there. His company was a small firm that dealt in futures. Mom cried a lot after he left the house. I remember watching her cry as she did the washing and wondering why. After all, my brother had hit her lots of times, and was always verbally abusing her. I wouldn't have blamed her if she'd been relieved to have him gone. I just couldn't understand why she should be sad. I was glad, myself. Finally, I thought, I didn't have to live in fear. While my brother was around, I had to always keep an eye on his mood."

"Was he that violent?"

"Once he snapped, he couldn't rein himself in. But that might run in the family. Dad's like that, too."

"I believe you'd told me your brother never married."

"That's correct. He was single to the end. Though he got the job in Nagoya, by the summer of the following year he'd quit and moved back in with us. After that it was just one job after another—he'd get hired, only to quit. The same thing over and over."

He'd hated his hometown, just hated it, and yet he'd waltz back home every time. That, too, was strange.

"What was the longest he ever held one job?"

"I guess about four years. That was a small loan operation in Shin Koiwa, in Tokyo. He seemed relatively healthy during that period. I was in high school, and during summer vacation I'd come to Tokyo and stay with him in his apartment. Once I entered high school, my brother seemed to be able to treat me as an equal, as another human being. He stopped terrorizing me. In fact, he was considerate, and at times dependent on me. But by the time I graduated and came to Tokyo, he'd already left that job."

Kunisada raised a hand gently, signaling for me to stop.

"I need to make sure of something. Why exactly did you come here today?"

"What do you mean, why did I come here?"

"In other words, what is it you'd like me to do?"

Shit. I'd talked for too long, and Kunisada was getting annoyed. His eyes were saying, *Hey, I'm not your therapist.*

"What is it I'd like you to do? Well, I'd like you to advise me."

"As a counselor, as a former academic advisor, or as a...friend?"

I took a deep breath and answered, choosing my words carefully, "I've come to my old college advisor to ask for guidance, of course."

Kunisada chuckled. "So, why do you finally need my help?"

I desperately cast about for the answer that would please

him just enough. "That's because nobody understands me like you do, Professor. After college, I started a career that has nothing to do with psychology or psychiatry. I've lost touch with all my old classmates. For several years now, I've been affiliated with a financial magazine as an editor-slash-writer— I've been thinking about nothing but markets and stocks and investments. There's nobody I can talk to about psychological problems. You're the only clinician I could think of that I could rely on."

"I see," Kunisada snorted. "Well, go on then."

"What else should I tell you about my brother?"

"In the end, when did your relationship with him change?"

"That would have been…about three years ago. He kept bouncing around from job to job, and going more and more to pieces mentally. Once he got into his late thirties, he couldn't even go out to work anymore. He just shut himself in his room at my parents' house, and his sleep schedule got turned around, and his eating habits became irregular. Little by little he started exhibiting signs of severe depression."

"Was a doctor consulted?"

"He absolutely refused to see one. And since he wasn't actually deranged, it would have been very difficult to take him in without his consent. Right around that time Mom began to develop neuroses from the pressure of having my brother around. So I took her to see a doctor and got my brother to accompany us. I'd already explained my brother's symptoms to the doctor and asked him to talk to my brother too."

"And what was the result?"

"He told me my brother had a personality disorder."

"I see."

"He said, 'This might sound strange, but it's not a mental illness. It's simply the personality your brother was born with. There's no way to treat it.'"

"An honest doctor."

"I'd had it, though. I told him, 'My brother's lifestyle is clearly that of a clinically depressed person.' And the doctor replied, 'You seem to have some knowledge of psychiatry. If you aren't satisfied with my diagnosis, feel free to see another doctor. If your brother were feeling worried about his inability to work, if he were seeking help, then I'd say he was suffering from depression. But at present, he doesn't seem to be suffering. He's living as he does because he chooses to. Unless he asks for help, how he lives is a question of personal preference.'"

"Well, he did have a point."

"The following year, Dad retired. He'd been a seaman, away most of the time, but now he was in the house. He took one look at my brother and exploded. To him it looked like my brother was just being lazy, sleeping all the time and never leaving the house. Well, from then on our family went downhill fast. My brother had always despised my father. He thought he was coarse and vulgar and resented his drinking. For his part, Dad would swear a blue streak at my brother, saying a man who doesn't work is a piece of shit. He was always preaching at him in that really negative way. Their mutual hatred grew, and pretty soon it was really bad. Of course, I didn't see it firsthand, since I was in Tokyo. But every time something happened, Mom would call me and give me a complete rundown. The conversations were totally one-sided: she'd talk and talk until I wondered when she'd quit, just a steady stream of complaints, until after a while she'd be so excited you could say she was in a frenzy. It really seemed that tensions had reached a critical point. Before long, my brother had begun to act out violently against Dad, and twice they had to call the police. Both times the police went away without doing anything, saying they didn't want to get involved in domestic matters. As a result of all this, Mom's blood pressure shot up to dangerous levels, so she left and went to stay with her younger sister in the Kansai region. That left just Dad and my brother in the house."

"A recipe for trouble." He was rubbing his jaw, a bitter look on his face. Another habit of his.

"Yes. Tensions rose higher and higher, and finally one night my father's nerves snapped, and in a fit of rage he cut my brother with a shard of glass. I got a call from the police and rushed home to find my brother still covered in blood. He was in his room, wrapped up in blankets and trembling. Dad was haggard from fear and fatigue—he looked stunned. I looked at the scene and realized that if I let things go on like that, one or the other was going to end up dead. So I persuaded my brother to come to Tokyo with me."

Kunisada interrupted me again. "Hold on. Are you telling

me that you took charge of him at that point?"

"Yes."

Silence.

"Why?" His voice as he asked this was different, stronger.

"I hoped to persuade him to see a therapist. As a last resort, I thought maybe I could counsel him myself."

"Impossible. Ninety-nine percent of attempts to counsel a family member fail. You know that. Granted, you were an excellent student with great potential, but you had no clinical experience. You were going to counsel a family member? That was rash of you."

"There was no other way."

"Why didn't you come to me?"

I'd considered it, any number of times. But I just couldn't. I was afraid of bringing my brother into contact with Kunisada. Taka would have figured out our past immediately. He had uncanny intuition.

"I couldn't come to you, Professor," I simply said.

"So why do you feel you can come to me now?"

"Well…"

Because I feel like I'm about to break down.

About three months after taking my brother in, I began to feel disturbed myself.

I couldn't stand the way he lived: aimlessly, with no prospects whatsoever. I wanted to yell at him like Dad did. Repressing that urge I began to feel as if some formless ugliness were eating away at the core of my being. I started to think that if I went on living with Taka I'd be the one to go mad.

From around February, I started not to come home to my apartment. I would sleep over with the guy I was seeing at the time. At first it was just once a week, but then it was once every three days, and finally I was only coming home when I needed to get something for work.

When I did come home, Taka would be there alone. He would have bought me a CD I wanted, or fixed the lock on the sliding-glass door. I'm sure it was just his clumsy way of showing me he meant well, but all it ever did was make me feel more gloomy.

I'd give him money. He'd buy piles of junk food and stacks of comics. I think he spent days on end in the apartment, just reading his comics. He'd try his best to do whatever I asked, but it depressed me to see the effort it cost him. His best intentions were always at cross-purposes, somehow. What was good for me never jived with what was good for him. Every pitch he threw came at my head.

And then one day I came home and he was gone.

I didn't search for him. I knew he didn't have any money, and I figured he was bound to come back soon. At the time, I didn't know that Taka had been cadging money from Dad. He'd called Dad and begged him, saying, "This time I'm really going to straighten out and look for a job." He'd asked for a million yen. Dad had given him I don't know how much. Dad told me then, "That's it. I'm cutting him off after this."

Once I learned that, I hurried to try and find Taka. I filed a missing person report. I tried to be optimistic—maybe he was actually trying to get back on his feet. Of course, what I was really thinking was how convenient it would be for me if he would.

His body was discovered two months after his disappearance. And I thought then that I'd known it would turn out that way.

After living with him for half a year, I'd had a foreboding: no matter how much I wanted things to turn out okay, they wouldn't. I didn't know why I'd had that feeling. In fact, I didn't know exactly what it was I'd felt or known. Or maybe I did but couldn't face it now. And what you hide from yourself holds you captive.

"You said you had a problem. But your brother is already dead. So what is it you need to talk to me about?"

"There are two things, actually," I answered, again choosing my words. "First, I haven't cried once since learning of my brother's death."

He nodded once, deeply.

"And the second thing is…a smell."

"A smell?"

"I smelled the smell of death in my brother's apartment, and ever since then, I've been extremely sensitive to smells. In particular, I pick up the smell of death everywhere. On people's breaths, on crowded trains, in parks, in downtown Shinjuku—everywhere, I detect particles of the scent that was coming from my brother's dead body."

"Have you considered the possibility that it's an olfactory hallucination?"

"I've considered it, but how would I know? I do know that it's the same smell. It's not like I've actually seen a corpse anywhere. Maybe there were buried ones nearby that I didn't see. It doesn't seem like a hallucination to me. But on the other hand, I know that, by definition, a hallucination doesn't seem like one. So I can't judge for myself."

After hearing me out, Kunisada put his hand to his forehead and thought for a while. Another favorite pose. People's habits really don't change. Whatever happened to the ten years that had elapsed? Sitting there facing him, it was as if time had been bent to make two of its ends meet.

"I think I understand what you're saying. And I think I understand what's bothering you, too. But it can't be resolved unless you figure it out for yourself, to your own satisfaction. What do you say to this? You're not my student anymore, but what if I became your therapist? One forty-five minute session a week. I'll even charge you. No contact whatsoever outside the counseling sessions. We can make a formal agreement, as counselor and patient. If you have no objections, I can set some time aside on Friday afternoons."

I looked up at him in surprise. "Really? You wouldn't mind?"

Kunisada had on his therapist face. He sounded serious. "However. You and I have a history. This is going to be tough for me. I might decide to abort the therapy. If I do, I'll introduce you to another analyst. Fair enough?"

I nodded.

"Yuki...no, I'd better call you Ms. Asakura. We'll start with an analysis of your dreams." Dream analysis was his specialty. "Bring a dream to next week's session. In addition, I'd like you to start thinking about how you interacted with your brother after you took him in. Write down whatever comes to you, but don't force it. Whatever happens to come to mind, no matter how minor, I want you to write it down then and there."

"Yes, Professor. Thank you very much."

"Well, then. I'll see you next week."

Kunisada showed me to the door, wearing his professional smile, the one that made him look like the host of a TV program. Feeling slightly hurt by his attitude, I bowed and left the room. And then I began to question why it should bother me that he was treating me professionally. I had come here harboring not the slightest fondness for the man—hadn't I?

Shit. I was already relying on him. That scared me. That's why relationships are dangerous.

7

I was exhausted. When I got home I lay down on the couch without changing. The late afternoon sun shone through the window. I picked up the remote and turned on the CD player. Vyatcheslav Kagan-Paley's *Ave Maria*.

High, fluffy clouds, dyed pink in the sunset. I fell asleep watching them cross the sky like a flock of rosy sheep.

The first thing I notice is a rundown wood-frame apartment building. The scene is a dim, cluttered back alley. Everything looks ancient. Everything feels shallow and unreal.

I remember now. I've seen this world in *Garo*, one of the comics mags my brother had been hooked on.

The apartment looks like one of those in which residents share toilets and sinks. My brother's room is on the first floor. It faces the sewer, and you can smell it even at the door. There's a rats' nest in the sewer drain, you can feel their beady little eyes staring at you.

My brother's is a dim, six-mat room. I'm seated facing him. We're talking. His bedding is in the corner. He never rolls it up. It's stained and faded. Three big spiders are plastered on the sliding closet doors like creatures from some shadow play.

I'm not in disguise or anything, but my brother is under the impression that I'm not his sister, but some other girl. And he seems to be interested in me sexually.

"You strange man, you," I laugh, elbowing him. I lean toward him ever so slightly, and he stiffens. He's kneeling formally.

"Come on, say something." I lay a hand on his knee. He smiles shyly, showing his missing front tooth.

All of a sudden I get my period.

I quickly fold up some toilet paper, but the wad is too big, and it slips out of place inside my underwear. I rip it in half. The half I throw away is leaching fresh blood onto the floor. I pick it up but the blood won't come off the bathroom floor.

As I stand there flustered, I can hear Taka outside bragging about me to a neighbor. "We're not exactly lovers, but I can't say I mind it when she comes over. I've got some ideas of my own, you know, and, well, if that's what she wants too, why not?"

His speech, as always, is self-involved and hard to follow, but you can tell he's happy to have a girlfriend. His girlfriend is his sister though, the idiot.

When Taka returns, I tell him I want to go buy sanitary napkins. "Let me tag along," he says, so off we go together. Of course, I don't want him with me, but he doesn't pick up on that.

There's a well next to the apartment building, as if it were some Edo-era rowhouse, and some neighborhood women are gathered around it with laundry. When I say hello, they all look startled and bow. They aren't real. They're comic-book women. Bucktoothed old ladies like the monster-loving *manga* artist Shigeru Mizuki would draw.

For some reason I'm beaming as I take his arm in mine. I parade him past the comic-book women with a defiant show of intimacy.

I bet you thought such a hopeless man would have to have a pretty pathetic girlfriend. Surprised to see me, *huh?* Such thoughts I think as I shower my brother with unnatural affection.

All of a sudden we're in a hot spring resort in the mountains. I've come up here with my brother and with a couple of friends of mine, a man and a woman. We're all having fun, but Taka's excitement seems rather unnatural. He's wearing a shabby old jacket and sits hunched over next to the heater.

I realize I haven't told my brother my name. He doesn't even know his lover's name. My friends call me "Yuki," and if either addresses me by name in the presence of my brother, even he'll figure out that I'm his little sister. I'm shit scared somebody might utter my name. But then why hasn't Taka asked his girlfriend her name? As soon as I think about it, I realize that I know the answer. But, I don't know what it is exactly.

Then it's time for bed.

Oh, no. I fret. I don't want to share a room with my brother. I frantically suggest a sleeping arrangement that will get me out of sleeping with him. "Um, we girls are going to sleep in this room. After all, she's not married—she can't share a room with a man she hardly even knows."

I look at my friend, but she's already curled up under the covers with the guy. Great, I think. There's no alternative.

I spread my futon out next to my brother's. I'm overcome with revulsion. I want to throw up.

Taka scoots over and puts his head on my shoulder. He wants to cuddle. His sticky, oily hair touches my cheek. He's acting like a little kid who wants a hug—I get goose bumps all over my body. Why doesn't this guy realize I'm his sister? Or is he just in denial?

Now I'm less grossed out than annoyed by his dimness. I want to shove him away. But I'm terrified of how he'll moan if I tell him I'm his sister. I'm stuck. I didn't mean to deceive him, but I did. I really regret it. I've really done it this time.

"Sorry, but I'm really tired. I'm going to sleep." I try to turn him down without seeming to, and turn my back to him. No response. I can hear his ragged breathing in the darkness. His eyes shone dully when I rejected him. He sensed something.

He has his doubts now. I'm his sister, I'm just pretending to be his girlfriend. But I don't look different, so why hasn't he noticed? I did it because I thought it would make him happy. I had no idea things would go this far. I'm worried sick about what'll happen when he finds out. But the more I try to hide it, the fishier it gets. Taka grows more reticent. If he realizes I'm his sister, he'll go crazy—he might even kill me.

I'm on the road near our home, walking toward the station. I'm trying hard to make conversation with my brother.

"Hey, Taka, what were you like when you were a kid?"

He doesn't answer. He looks angry.

"You were really cute as a child," I say to take up the slack. Then I gasp. I know things I shouldn't know; it's only because I'm his little sister that I've seen photos of him as a child. He *was* a cute kid. He had a smile that made him look totally different from the way he is now. That I know. And now I've let him know I know.

I'm terrified. I can't look at him.

Still I can feel his anger and despair. Little black bugs crawl out of him, covering his face and his body. *A visual image of his despair*, I think.

I glance over and—what the...? He's shrinking before my eyes. Fast. Now he's down to three feet, now a foot, until finally he's only a few inches tall. He could stand on my hand.

What's going on? Why?

I pick up my shrunken brother and set him on the palm of my hand. He just lies there. I can feel the weight of his body on my hand. He's soft, like a dead cat. He might die. He could die any moment now. I have to do something. I start to fret. I've got to send for help right away.

I rush to a pay phone in the station. I drop twenty yen in and call 911. The operator comes on the line. I tell her I need an ambulance.

She says, "Response time is slow right now because of the fog. One'll be there in about thirty minutes."

I feel rage welling up inside me. I can't wait that long. "Go to hell!" I yell, and slam down the receiver.

Taka's just lying there in my hand, limp. What should I do? I need to get him to a hospital. I decide to take him to a psychiatric ward. What else can I do for him? So I decide after all to call an ambulance. I go to a different pay phone.

I pick up the receiver and a voice says, "Well now, that's Yuki, isn't it?"

What? I haven't even dialed yet. "Yes, it is. Who are you?"

The lines are crossed. My outgoing call is getting crossed with a call coming in for me. The voice is the switchboard operator, and she's trying to connect me to an incoming call. But I want to call out.

"Please, let me make this call!" I scream.

There's still time, if I can get through right now. If I try once more and be really nice to him and take really good care of him, I know my brother will grow back to his original size. I'm sure of it. If I give him lots of love and pay him lots of attention he'll return to normal, that's all. There's still time. I hug my shrunken brother to my chest and murmur—*pray*—

There's still time. There's still time.

I glance down and see a small white plug dangling from my brother's body like a bird's foot.

8

The dream was shattered by the ringing of the telephone.

In a haze, I picked up the receiver. "Hello?"

It was Kimura, the cameraman. "Yuki? Were you asleep?"

"Yeah."

"Is everything okay?"

"Yeah. I was dreaming, that's all."

Echoes of the dream were still with me. Taka, shrunken, lying on the palm of my hand. The frustration of not being able to get the call through. That odd plug.

"Would you like to have dinner this evening?"

The plug. The *plug*...

"Are you listening to me? Hey."

"Huh? Oh, um, sure. Dinner. Where?"

He named a European-style eatery in Shibuya. I wrote down the location and the time.

"Listen..." I said.

"What?"

"What do you think of when you hear the word 'plug'?"

Kimura fell silent, confused: what the hell was I talking about?

"I just had a dream about one." I was still vaguely ruminating about the images I'd seen in my dream.

"A plug, huh?" Then he said, "A television set, maybe?"

"Anything else?"

"Hmm. Just appliances, I guess. Maybe a vacuum cleaner."

The vacuum cleaner that had been left outletted in my brother's room.

"Thanks. See you at seven."

After I had showered and changed, I stopped by the video-rental place near my apartment.

I hadn't been there in a while. They'd remodeled and increased their shelf space and installed one of those big, showy sensor contraptions by the door. My pulse quickens when I know I'm being monitored. It's like that at the automatic styles at the train station; I always get really tense when I go through them.

I go to the foreign classics corner, hoping they have what I'm looking for.

Mondo Cane.

Thanks to my nap, I recalled that my brother had mentioned a certain scene from *Mondo Cane* several times. It had slipped my mind, but that plug hanging from my brother's body had brought it back.

Mondo Cane came out years ago. I didn't know when exactly my brother had seen it, but he'd have been in high school when it was playing in theaters. The theme song had been a big hit. I was only in grade school, but I still remembered the song, a beautiful tune called "More."

I scanned the titles on the shelf, and found *Mondo Cane* almost immediately. I found three of them, in fact: there were two sequels. I hesitated for a moment, then took all three tapes to the counter. One of them might hold the key to understanding my brother's death. Still, what a title—*A Dog's World*. The Japanese translation was worse—*Cruel Tales from around the World*. I was depressed already.

I put the blue plastic bag containing the videos into my shoulder bag and headed to Shibuya.

I don't really like Shibuya. Walking around in that district gives me a headache. The Shibuya station sits in a little valley surrounded by hills, and it makes me feel like I'm at the bottom of a grinding bowl—I get claustrophobic there. The place where we were meeting was a little ways up one of those hills, Dogenzaka; I felt relief as I went up the hill and the crowd thinned out.

It was a bistro on the first-floor of a mixed-occupancy building. Kimura had arrived early. He was sitting at a table by the window, gazing out, looking oddly rigid. His camera bag was on the seat beside him; evidently he was on the way home from work. He had a navy-blue baseball cap with gold laurel leaves stitched onto the bill pulled down over his eyes. He was the kind of guy whose simplicity was obvious just from looking at him. It made me uneasy. I feel more comfortable with more convoluted types. Kimura was always polite. Too polite—he always seemed a little wet behind the ears. Maybe his politeness was what kept him from really succeeding as a photographer. Creative people seem more talented if they come across as uninhibited, even a little selfish.

"Sorry. Did you wait long?" I asked him. For a split second, I thought about the smell, but I brushed the thought away. I'd ignore it.

"No, no, I just got here. Did you have any trouble finding the place?"

"None at all."

Menus appeared, and we chose the food and wine. When we looked up, we were face to face. Head-on, Kimura looked more childlike than his thirty-three years warranted.

"Are you feeling better?"

"Mostly."

"That's good. You know, you started talking about smells when I was over at your place last time. Made me self-conscious. I started worrying if I smelled bad—I went right home and took a bath!"

I laughed. "I'm so sorry about that. That was pretty rude, wasn't it, to start talking about odors all of a sudden."

"I have to confess, I haven't been to a doctor yet."

"Cut it out. You don't need to see one. It was just me. So much happened, I think the stress just got me, that's all. Forget about it, okay?"

He flashed me a sympathetic smile. We raised our wine glasses for a toast, and made idle conversation about work as we ate. Then, when we were starting to feel sated, Kimura got down to business.

"So, what do you think? Do you wanna get married?"

I thought I'd heard wrong. "Huh?"

"I asked, do you want to get married?"

"Married?"

"Yeah."

"To whom?"

"To me, that's who."

I couldn't hold it in. I burst out laughing. "Come off it. What's wrong with you?"

"Nothing's wrong with me. I've liked you for a long time. I've always hoped for a chance to have a serious relationship with you, and I feel this is it. You know, when you came on to me, I really didn't know what to do. Part of me was thrilled, because I'd had my eye on you for so long, but part of me was afraid that if we slept together right then, that's as far as it'd ever go. I thought about it a lot, trying to figure out what I could say to make you come around. And then before I'd made up my mind, your brother passed away, so unexpectedly, and it became even harder to say anything to you. I mean, right after a girl's come back from the funeral of a family member is not exactly the perfect time to woo her. But I was afraid I'd lose my chance if I let too much time go by. I know it doesn't make any sense to you. And I don't expect you to marry me right away. All I'm suggesting is that we start dating with marriage in mind. I'm saying this because I'm afraid that otherwise, you'll go on dodging me forever."

He seemed serious. I sighed. What the hell was this guy thinking?

"Listen, you know me pretty well, right?" I said.

"Yeah."

"So, you must know what kind of girl I am. You know what everybody thinks of me. How can you want to marry me?"

He glared at me angrily. "You're talking about your being a flirt?"

"What else could I be talking about? You know how loose I am. I'm the notorious slut who sleeps with everybody she works with. You saw me drunk the other night, right? That's me. Or maybe you think you're doing the responsible thing, is that it? Look, I hardly even remember it, so don't make a big thing out of it."

I thought myself that I'd spoken a little too brazenly, but the words had just come out.

"Would you please not talk that way? Because nobody talks that way about you. You're being paranoid. You're not being fair to the people around you."

"Well, excuse me, then."

I gulped some water.

"Sure, you're kind of weird. Even then, I'm crazy about you. I think I know you pretty well, Yuki, and have for a long time. Five years. And as far as I know, you're a good person. You're bright and cheerful and you're fun to be around. You're popular with guys. It's always you who seduces them, and you who ditches them, but I don't think that makes you loose or bad or anything. You say the only thing you're interested in is stocks. Is there a woman in the world like that? And yet you're not interested in money. I can't tell if you're kind or nasty. I can't figure out what you're thinking. But I can't just sit by and watch you. It hurts. And if it's going to hurt anyway, then I might as well be with you. Watching you from a distance, I just end up consumed with worry. So just shut up and be with me already."

He looked like he was struggling to be cheerful.

"No way."

"Why not?"

"I don't even like you, that's why."

It was true.

"Give it time. You will."

"I won't."

"How do you know?"

"Because you're too good. You're boring."

"Don't be mean."

"No, I think I'd better come right out and say it."

"You don't have to give me your answer right away."

"You're an idiot. I'm getting out of here."

I grabbed my purse and stood up. I almost ran out of the bistro. I could hear him calling after me, but I didn't look back. I was too shaken.

Was I that unstable? Was I so fucked up that Kimura felt he couldn't leave me on my own? I thought I knew myself pretty well, but was that how I looked to other people? I felt antsy, as if people were seeing through me. I knew that something was out of whack. Everything felt all mixed up. Nothing fit quite right. I wasn't ever good at living, but I'd thought I was doing a pretty good job of hiding it, of passing. But I was actually so screwed up that even clueless Kimura was worried about me.

I made my way down Dogenzaka. The sticky Shibuya heat wrapped itself around me, covering me in a film. It was hot. Why did this place have to feel so nasty? When I got to the bottom of the hill, I stopped in my tracks.

There it was again. The smell.

The magenta night sky was closing in on me. I looked around, searching for the source. I was jostled by the throngs, countless men and women, boys and girls, hair dyed every conceivable shade, legs bared, chests half-uncovered, breath spewing from each mouth, innumerable odors rising from the mass of bodies. The ground suddenly turned soft and squishy, and my knees began to give way. I could smell it. I could definitely smell it. Decomposing flesh. I didn't know where it was coming from. I had a feeling it was from way up Center Avenue, with all its shops and crowds. No, the whole area was suffused with the stench of dead bodies. I wanted to vomit. My legs felt so weak I couldn't stay standing.

Just when I was about to collapse, somebody grabbed my arm from behind. I turned around: it was Kimura. The reek assailed me again. "Are you all right?" As his lips formed the words, the stench of rotting fish spilled from his mouth. Terrified, I pushed him away and fled as fast as I could.

9

"And how are you feeling?"

Kunisada spoke calmly, and he stared at me as he spoke. He was seated comfortably on his sofa, hands clasped on one knee, as usual. I took a deep breath, closed my eyes, and tried to gather my thoughts. So that I could just *be* in front of Kunisada, right now, at this very moment—as honestly, openly, and straightforwardly as possible.

"Three days ago, in Shibuya, I had a slight panic attack," I answered, choosing my words carefully.

"Tell me more."

"I was walking down the street, and suddenly I smelled death."

"That's all?"

I hesitated.

"If you don't want to tell me, you don't have to."

"I'd been with a certain man."

"So you had gotten together with a man that day." Kunisada's tone didn't waver. He spoke kindly, receptively, just like the books said to.

"He proposed to me."

"Proposed?"

"Yes. But it wasn't what I wanted, so I turned him down. I turned him down, left the restaurant, and was walking alone when I smelled it. I stopped, and he grabbed my arm."

"So he had followed you."

"And the guy…smells like death. Always."

"Always?"

"Yes. Well, at least he did the last time I'd seen him. And this time too."

"And that's what brought on the attack?"

"Probably."

"Hmm…Is this difficult for you, by the way?"

"I'm all right for now. I'm calm."

"So the smell comes from this man's body?"

"Yes…from his mouth."

"Is it a strong smell?"

"No, it's very faint, just a few particles. It's diffused and mixed in with several layers of odor."

"Do you pick this odor up on anyone besides this man?"

"Sometimes. I feel like I'm getting more attuned to it all the time. On the way here today, I became aware of it all of a sudden in the middle of a residential neighborhood. It was just an average neighborhood, a street lined with houses that all looked the same. It smelled more like rotting blood than a corpse, I guess. Maybe a cat had died in somebody's yard."

"Are you able to sleep?"

"Yes."

"So there's no sleep disorder involved."

"No."

"Have you had any dreams since we saw each other last week?"

"I have…"

"Would you like to talk about your dreams?"

I reached into my purse and took out the memo pad on which I'd been writing down my dreams. He flipped through the pages of the dream journal until he came to the page with the heading *A Dream about my Brother Shrinking*.

"Last week, after we spoke, I went home and dozed off. That was the dream I had then, a very vivid dream. I dreamed that I was deceiving my brother by pretending to be his girl-friend."

"And your brother shrank."

"Right."

Recalling it was unpleasant.

"So how do you feel about this dream?"

"I think it's the truth. I did resort to a kind of erotic method to get close to my brother in the end. I used sexuality to try to give him strength. In other words, I think what the dream was telling me was that I played the role of lover to breathe life into him, and failed. That's how it seems to me."

"Why do you think that?"

"When I asked my brother to leave the house and move in with me, it was like I was proposing to him. 'Hey, let's make a go of this together. Everything'll work out fine,' I was telling him—very earnestly, sincerely. And I finally persuaded my brother, who never set foot outside his room, to leave the house."

"You feel like you seduced him?"

"Right. When I was trying to convince him, I feel like I made use of the fact that I'm a woman, used it to a shocking degree. I knew if I didn't he'd never manage to drag himself out of there."

Kunisada nodded. "I understand your thinking. Even though you were his little sister, to your brother you were also an attractive member of the opposite sex. It was a risky strategy, but with a high chance of success."

"I couldn't think of any other way. And I thought my family would start killing each other if I didn't do something quick."

When he first arrived at my place, I'd prepared clothing and pajamas and toiletries for my brother. I'd gotten everything ready for him, like some paramour.

Physically, he was in rotten shape. He didn't have enough psychological stamina left at that point to keep himself clean. It takes a healthy ego to maintain personal hygiene. It looked like he hadn't washed his face or brushed his teeth in months. Two front teeth had been eaten away by too many soda drinks. It looked like his liver was going—his complexion was bad, and he had eczema on his face. A year of nocturnal living and not taking care of himself had sapped his strength. His skin was dry and cracked, and his eyes were yellow and cloudy. He lived on Coke and junk food—if he ate anything else he just barfed it up.

I changed his clothes for him and forced him into the

bathtub. At first he resisted, but I reasoned with him gently until he sulked his way in. I can only imagine how much mental energy it must have taken him to come all the way over to my place and then take a bath. As much energy as it would take any normal person to climb Mt. Everest, probably. To help him summon the strength, I treated him as kindly as a girlfriend. Unconsciously. I dried him off with a towel, blow-dried his hair. He was surprisingly passive. Childlike. And that's how our life together began.

Kunisada let out a sigh.

The afternoon sun shone through the blinds. It was too quiet. This counseling room was always too quiet. Staring at the cream-colored walls, I began to feel foolish. The room was too silent and too clean, and I didn't like it.

"Do you mind if I ask you about the man who proposed to you?" Elbows on his desk, chin resting on his hands, Kunisada gazed at me. "You say you turned him down. In which case, I wonder why he proposed to you. Surely he had some kind of expectation that you might accept."

"I have no idea. We've been friends for a long time, but I had no clue he was thinking of marriage."

"So this was all something he'd conjured up in his head?"

"Well…maybe not entirely. I might have done something to give him the wrong idea."

"Something to give him the wrong idea?"

"Well, I…that is…I got drunk one night and slept with him."

"You seduced him?"

"I didn't mean to."

"But in the end, that's what happened."

"I guess."

Silence reigned for a while. I thought for a while about the word "seduced." Was that what I'd done to Kimura?

"You are quite the temptress, Yuki," Kunisada muttered.

"A temptress? Me?"

"Yes, you."

"Why? How?"

Kunisada remained silent and shook his head, as if to say, I think you know. Had I seduced Taka and Kimura both? As I pondered the two of them in turn, an eerie thought came to me.

Now that I thought about it, there was something about Kimura that reminded me of my brother.

"Why don't we call it a day?" Kunisada stood and opened the door, as if to chase me out. We were on the new campus now, and the hallway sparkled.

"Next week I'd like to hear a little more about your life with your brother."

I nodded and bowed. "Goodbye, then," he said, and shut the door. Wham. As I stared at the blank white door, drops of bitterness were forming in me. I was seized with the impulse to beat down the door. I forced my arms down.

10

I must have fallen asleep. The clock read eight, it was already evening. On days I talked to Kunisada I always came back tired and went right to sleep. I felt like I'd been dreaming, but I couldn't recall what about.

Eight o'clock. Kind of an in-between time. The thought of staying home alone gave me a weird, lonesome feeling, like the world had forgotten about me. I wanted company. I wanted to lay my head on some guy's chest and doze while he caressed my hair. I needed someone else's body to make sure mine existed. If I caved in to the mood, I'd end up roving the city at night looking for a man. I was sure of it. In the emotional state I was in I was bound to sleep with the first guy I came across, and that wouldn't do me any good. Something in me was warning against that course. If I didn't restrain myself, I'd lose all control.

I took my bottle of zubrovka from the freezer and had a swallow. The mouthwash taste of the liquid cleared my head.

Right. I should watch the videos. I had to find the scene in *Mondo Cane* that had so fascinated my brother. I took the first cassette from the blue plastic bag and inserted it into the VCR.

It was just one disconcerting image after another. I watched it in search mode, double time, so I could keep an eye out for the scene he'd described. But I got to the end without finding it. There was no such scene in *Mondo Cane*. Maybe he'd imagined it.

I popped in *Mondo Cane 2*. Scenes of aboriginal religious rites and animal sacrifice. Not what I was looking for. I put the third tape in. My eyes were getting tired.

Sipping my zubrovka on the rocks, I watched, still in search mode. Suddenly the scene shifted to a hospital room. I quickly pushed PLAY.

The camera slowly panned until a lone boy appeared on the left edge of the screen. The film quality wasn't very good—it looked like a home movie. The boy was about twelve years old and white.

An aged nurse was motioning to him. The boy stood stock-still like a doll. The nurse called and called, but he gave no sign of responding. As though his spirit had abandoned his body, he just stood there in front of the dingy wall of the sickroom. The camera was trained directly on the boy now, looking him full on in the face. His eyes were vacant, holes in a dead tree. His hand clenched a thin cord. The end of it dragged on the floor. On the end was a white plug.

The nurse said something, and then plugged the cord into the outlet.

Suddenly the boy moved. He came to life and began to look around him.

There was a voice-over. "This schizophrenic boy can only

come alive when he is connected to a source of electricity."

This was it. This boy was what my brother had told me about.

Hey, Yuki. You know that movie, Mondo Cane? *I saw it a long time ago, but there's one scene I can't forget. There's this schizophrenic boy in it. This boy, he can't move unless you plug him in. When you disconnect him, he just stops moving. Why? How did he get like that? How are that boy and his outlet connected? I can't figure it out. Yuki, is schizophrenia genetic? You know a lot about that stuff—tell me. That kid who can't live unless he's plugged in—is it his fault? Is it his parents' fault? What went wrong? Was it fate—was he just born that way? Why can't he live without his outlet? Why?*

Taka, mental illness does have a genetic component, but that doesn't account for everything. In fact, the mechanism that causes mental illness to develop isn't fully understood yet. We haven't solved the riddle of why people go mad. That's more or less how I answered him, but what he was really asking me was, why is it so hard for me, Taka, to live? But I didn't have an answer to that. *I just don't know. Nobody will ever know. Finding the answer to that is what life is all about, right?* Maybe I said something like that.

Maybe the reason I'd been stuck on the vacuum cleaner in my brother's apartment was that I'd heard him talk about this boy. The information in my subconscious had been stirred up by the sight of the vacuum.

The boy on the video seemed to think of himself as some kind of machine powered by electricity. He'd denied his humanity and chosen to live as a machine. Why? Probably because it was easier for him that way. But, why? What cause could produce such an effect? There was no way of knowing.

Maybe my brother pulled the plug on himself.

When he'd outletted the vacuum, he'd flashed back to the boy in the movie. At that instant, my brother no longer knew why he had to go on as a human being. To vacuum the apartment, to keep the apartment, to keep living in this world—he could no longer see the need for any of it. And so he unplugged himself.

But then, what did plugs really stand for? What did outlets mean to my brother—to the boy? What did they gain?

The phone was ringing.

I came to my senses, startled. The video had ended and the VCR had shut off. The screen was showing a regular TV program. I jumped to my feet to grab the receiver. I had a slight headache. I'd been concentrating so hard on my own thoughts that reality was out of perspective for me now. Kimura's too lively voice spoke into my ear. I found it somehow unpleasant.

"What?"

"Don't get so mad at me, Yuki. You're hurting me already."

"Well, what do you expect, after what you said last time I saw you?"

"Sorry about that. Did you get home okay?"

"Of course I did. I'm here, aren't I?"

Why was I so angry?

"Listen, I wanted to call right away, but you gave me such a nasty look, and you pushed me away like that.... I didn't have the courage. You gave me quite a shock."

But now he sounded as cheerful as though nothing had happened. I was angry because he'd invaded my private world. I had to work hard to tune in to the frequency of his voice now. What a pain in the ass.

"I wasn't feeling well—something was wrong with me. Don't let it bother you." I felt guilty for running away from him.

"Hey, no problem. I went home and did a lot of thinking."

"About what?"

"Well, there I was saying how worried I was about you, and I let myself get discouraged just because you glared at me and pushed me away. How do I expect to be able to take care of you like that? So I'm not going to hesitate anymore. I'm going to stick with you no matter how much you hate me. If I don't I'll lose you. For the first time in a long time, I felt really disgusted by my own weakness."

I couldn't keep myself from guffawing. I'd caught the frequency.

"Were you always like this, Kimura? I never expected this."

"You think of me as a pretty good guy. But you're wrong."

"Is that so?"

"I'm not just pretty good, I'm ridiculously good."

"Ha, ha, ha."

"Good to hear you laugh."

"Hey…Listen."

"What?"

"If we get serious, I might really hurt you. That's what I'm afraid of."

"Yeah?"

"Don't call me anymore."

"I will call you. I have the right to get hurt." Then he added, "I don't know what it is you're carrying around inside, Yuki, but I'm going to help you. I don't know what I can do, but I want to do something. Whatever you're facing, I'll face it too. Trust me. Alone, you'll be crushed. I realized that when we were together for the first time."

I couldn't figure out what he meant by that.

"Did I do something that night when I was drunk?"

"Nothing much."

"Come on, tell me what the fuck happened!" I yelled into the receiver.

"If I tell you, then we're in it together. Agreed? You can't avoid me anymore. Promise me."

"Okay, okay. I promise. Now tell me."

Kimura took a deep breath and spoke. "That night, in bed, you were staring at a corner of the ceiling and muttering. You said…your brother was there, watching you."

Beyond the unmanned railroad crossing, my brother turned toward me, and was gone.

11

I'm alone in a cave, bathing in a dark pool.

Where is this? I can hear the *splat*, *splat* of water dripping from the rock ceiling. The cave's interior is lit by flickering candlelight. The water is hot and murky. Ah, it's a dream. I'm dreaming again. That's all I seem to do lately. The line between dream and reality is starting to blur. I don't even know which is which anymore. My dreams are rupturing, leaking out.

I decide it's about time to get out. I wade through the water toward the mouth of the cave. In a dilapidated changing-room I put on a cotton bathrobe.

The place seems to be a hot spring. But which one? I fasten my robe and walk down the inn's dark, narrow hallway. There I run into Kunisada.

He's wearing a bathrobe too. He flashes me a grin. He wraps an arm around my waist and pulls me toward him.

"Professor, no! The others will find out!"

"Don't worry about that," he says, trying to kiss me.

"Stop!" I try to shake free of him, but he won't let go. The front of my robe has come loose, and his fingers are crawling up my thighs.

"Professor, we're starting," cries a female student.

It's Ritsuko Honda. That's right, I'm on a trip with the other psych majors. I can't be doing this.

I rush into a classroom to find the other students all there, preparing to give their reports. I'm the only one in a bathrobe—I feel totally out of place. While I stand there trying to decide if I should go back and change, Professor Kunisada enters. Also in a robe. Everybody looks at us strange. I'm embarrassed.

I am being caressed by Kunisada, again.

He's on top of me, licking my nipples tenaciously. The floor mats are cool against my cheek. Kunisada takes care to lick each nipple the same number of times. "You wouldn't want one to get smaller than the other, would you?" he says, working his tongue in deep concentration, like a child sucking on hard candy.

There's something cute about him, I think. But there are other places I wish he'd lick, too. I'm horny now, and sopping wet. I want to touch myself, but I can't bring myself to do something so shameful. I wish he'd just put his finger inside me.

"Now spread your legs," he commands me.

I feel like rebelling. "No."

"I won't lick you, then."

"I don't want you to."

But something's funny, and I'm laughing. Something tells me my classmates are about to file in. I can't let them find me like this. Quickly, I sit up and start to do up my robe again. Kunisada loses his head and hides in a closet, for some reason.

The paper door rattles open and five or six students come in, talking among themselves. Their leader is Ritsuko Honda. The minute she enters the room she senses, with her usual sharp intuition, that something is wrong. Suspicious, she looks around the room, and then drops her gaze to where I'm rearranging the front of my robe. There's disdain in her eyes, like she knows all about Kunisada and me.

Everybody in the room starts talking pleasantly, and then for some reason Kunisada, in the closet, starts banging away with a hammer. The *thwack, thwack* of his blows rings out over our heads.

"Hey, what's that noise?" Ritsuko starts to look around.

Thwack, thwack, thwack, thwack.

Everybody falls silent. Ritsuko looks straight at me.

I realize that everybody's guessed the truth about me and the Professor. An idea comes to me and I turn toward the closet. That's when I say it.

"Professor, would you please explain to everyone your relationship with me?"

The hammering stops. I wait, nervous about how he'll respond. Finally, from inside the closet, he says:

I haven't gone all the way with Yuki.

12

"Isn't there something else you'd like to tell me?"

The session was nearly over. Kunisada forced a smile as he asked me the question.

"Why do you ask?"

"No reason. Just a hunch."

He was right, of course. There was still one thing I hadn't told him. I shifted in my chair, took a deep breath, and confessed. "I had a dream about you, Professor."

He leaned forward. "Is that so? What kind of dream?"

"I dreamed that we were having sex."

Now it was his turn to shift in his chair.

"Can you talk about it?"

I nodded, and started to tell him the content of the dream. In minute detail. Kunisada listened with his eyes closed, head down. He didn't seem shocked.

"You answered that you hadn't gone all the way with me yet. All I heard was your voice from inside the closet. Then the dream ended."

I was trying to speak calmly, but I could feel my armpits breaking out in a sweat. Kunisada's eyes opened a crack, and he gave a derisive laugh.

"It would seem you still didn't trust me in the least," he said. His fingers were toying with a paperweight. It was made of brass and shaped like an angel.

"Hmm. You may be right. I still don't trust you, Professor."

"Do you want to continue, in spite of that?"

He let the angel fall with a thud onto the desktop. I couldn't answer. Silence. The air conditioner droned on.

"Do you…Professor, you don't hate me?"

There, I'd finally put it into words: the thing I'd most wanted to ask, but hadn't been able to. What kind of feelings, exactly, did this man harbor for me now? I wanted to know. After all, maybe he was only meeting with me in order to get revenge. I couldn't shake the suspicion. What if, after I opened up to him, he shoved me away? I might go insane.

For a moment he seemed to be at a loss for words. Then, he blushed slightly and stroked his chin. Which was what he did when he was about to confess something.

"Well, I can't say I don't hate you."

Now his fingers were slowly caressing the angel's wings. "I suffered a great deal of pain on your account, you know. Heartbreak in middle age can be rather severe. To be frank, Yuki, I had always been faithful to my wife—you were the first woman I'd had an affair with in all that time. I never foresaw getting into a situation like that, where I couldn't turn back, but I was into you body and soul. I lost all reason. I was forty then, coming up on the autumn of my life. It's embarrassing to have to admit it, but I was trying to live out fantasies of the romantic fulfillment that I hadn't experienced in my youth. Logically, of course, I knew that. But heartbreak is a kind of identity crisis, and that's what I went through. I think it was a valuable experience. It taught me just how painful the collapse of the ego can be. To be honest, it gives me great pain to see you. Those feelings of betrayal still remain somewhere in the bottom of my heart."

I pressed, "In that case, why did you agree to counsel me?"

He leaned forward and fixed me with a stern look. "I'm a doctor. When I see that someone is suffering, that's everything to me. You were right here in front of me, suffering, and that had to take priority. That's how bad you looked at that moment, that's all."

For some reason he was making my skin creep.

He continued, "In the same way that you don't trust me, I don't trust you. At the moment, we're still traveling parallel courses."

"I guess so…"

After a long silence, Kunisada stood up and said, "I think we'd better leave it there for today."

It was true that I didn't trust Kunisada. There were things I couldn't tell him. The fact that I'd seen my brother at the railroad crossing, for instance. The fact that I'd seen my brother, apparently, the night I slept with Kimura. I kept going in circles in my head about whether or not to tell him.

If I did, how would he respond? Rationality dictated that those encounters had to be illusions conjured up by my own psyche. Silly shadows, or tricks of the light, that I'd mistaken for my brother. Why? Because, most likely, I'd been unconsciously worrying about Taka for a long time. As an explanation, that was extremely persuasive.

I already knew the answers that psychology had to offer. In which case, was there any point in posing the questions?

I used a pay phone on campus to check my messages. I don't generally use cell phones. If I hold one to my ear for three minutes or so, the electromagnetic waves give me a headache. I hear a constant, low buzz, like an insect in my ear canal, and then all the nerves in my temples and sinuses begin to feel like they're going into convulsions.

I had several messages from work. It was about time I got serious about my job again. Mourning be damned, if I kept turning down assignments they'd stop coming. I was well aware of that, but still I couldn't face the thought of going out on a story. I was having an editorial colleague pinch-hit for me on the monthly column I was responsible for, but if I failed to take care of it next month, too, I'd probably be taken off of it and lose half my income.

I knew I had to get myself out of this situation somehow, and quick. It wasn't that there was anything specifically wrong with me. Just a mild depression. Worrying about it, trying to push myself out of it, wouldn't do any good. I knew that. I had all the answers.

I was strolling across campus listening to the murmur of

the cicadas when someone slapped me on the back. I turned around, and there was Ritsuko Honda, in a white lab coat. For a moment, as I stared at her face, dream and reality merged.

"Yuki Asakura? Oh my God, how long has it been? Do you remember me? We were in the same class—Ritsuko Honda."

It was her. In the flesh.

"Of course I remember you. How've you been?"

Her smile seemed overly familiar to me. I was taken aback, wondering if I had once been very close to her and it had just slipped my mind.

"What are you doing here?"

We both said this at the same time, and we broke up laughing. Then she took me inside one of the buildings, to a corner by some vending machines, and invited me to take a seat. There was no air conditioning and it was sweltering.

As she fed coins into a machine, Ritsuko spoke to me as if I were some long-lost friend. "Actually, I ended up switching to cultural anthropology. I moved on to the graduate program here and did three years of fieldwork in Okinawa. I just came back last year and now I'm Professor Kitamura's research assistant."

Gradually my memories of Ritsuko were becoming less vague. Now that I thought about it, my feelings toward her had always been complicated. Ritsuko had always been clear-headed, the type of person who always had her eyes fixed on her goals. She never got confused. She came on like a big sister, very centered, and in time all her classmates came to trust her. Totally unlike me.

"Yuki, I seem to remember hearing you went into journalism," she said, a note of hesitation in her voice.

"Nothing grand—I'm just a freelance writer. And I ended up specializing in finance. Nothing I studied in school has turned out to be of any use whatsoever." And now I was this close to being out of work.

"That's a surprise. I always thought you'd end up doing something related to psychology. You had a real feel for it— and you were Professor Kunisada's star pupil."

I gave a noncommittal response. She probably knew everything. That's why she appeared in my dream. There was no point in hiding anything now.

"I ended up experiencing a case of transference with Professor Kunisada. There was a lot of trouble, and I couldn't control myself. So I quit. I figured I wasn't qualified to handle other people's psyches."

"*Really*? Is that what happened? I sort of figured something like that was going on."

It suddenly hit me that ten years had gone by. And now I was able to sit here and calmly discuss something like this with Ritsuko.

"People knew, didn't they?"

"Well, they suspected, vaguely. It was quite a shock to the boys. I mean, they all had crushes on you, Yuki."

Now, that was a surprise. I'd never had the slightest inkling of that.

"You've got to be kidding," I said. "None of them ever hit on me."

"That's because you were so unapproachable. Even to a girl like me, you always seemed like a real *femme fatale*."

"Knock it off, you're embarrassing me."

A *femme fatale*? Me? Unbelievable. At the time, I was always on edge, and I'd just figured nobody wanted to have anything to do with me, especially after I started seeing Kunisada.

"I mean…everybody disapproved of me."

"Come on, you're being paranoid. Everybody was fascinated by you, everybody wanted to know what you were thinking. They just found it hard to strike up a conversation with you. They were all young and self-conscious, you know. Me, too—I don't mind confessing, now, that I really thought you were interesting."

I was floored. I had never dreamed that Ritsuko had noticed me. I'd always thought she wouldn't want anything to do with me.

"You don't have to look so shocked. I don't mean it in a bad way. How shall I put it? There was always something special about you, Yuki. I think everybody felt it."

"Special? Me?"

"Yes. Hmm…I think the time I felt so the most was when we all went on that retreat to study treatment methods. Remember? We went to the mountains up in Nagano to do role-play therapy."

Now that she mentioned it, I did remember a retreat like that. We'd stayed for a couple of nights. I'd been in a bad mood the whole time. The participants were mostly mental health professionals of one sort or another, all very generous and quick on the uptake. People who spend their lives trying to peer into other people's psyches tend to share a certain unique hypocrisy. They pride themselves on being able to manipulate people, and they apply their perceptiveness to hiding it. I remembered now: that was when I'd decided I couldn't remain in that world forever.

"I watched you take part in a workshop during the retreat," Ritsuko continued. "Remember the one on psychodrama? People who decide to go into the mental health field tend to have issues themselves, right? And on 'research' retreats like that, their own problems tend to spill out—no matter how much they pretend it's just an exercise. It's only natural, of course: we can only relate to other people's psyches through our own problems. Anyway, one of the participants broke down right in the middle of the workshop, just went delusional. The facilitator inadvertently touched on some personal trauma of hers. It's easy to do if you're not sensitive. Anyway, some sort of complex in her subconscious was stimulated all of a sudden, and she started to get excited. The anger started welling up from the depths of her mind like lava or something, and there was no way to stop it. Once she broke down, that was it. All of her past resentments started flowing through this breach in her psyche. An acute case if there ever was one. And there were twenty professional counselors there, all lined up like ducks in a row, and none of them could quiet her—they were all too self-conscious in front of each other. And then you stepped forward. And everybody yielded to you, even though you were still a student and they were all pros. It was quite a sight. You walked slowly up to the delusional woman, and you knelt and took her hands, and it looked almost as if you were trying to synchronize yourself with the rhythms of her breathing and blinking. I'll never forget the way she looked when you approached her. She gazed at you as if you were a goddess or something. As if she were supplicating to you for aid. You held her head to your breast, like you would a child, and you started stroking her back, like this. Almost as if you were brushing her anger off to the ground. You seemed almost to be releasing all the rage from inside her. I swear, I had chills running up my spine, just watching you. I thought, 'This girl's a genius when it comes to fully accepting other people.' If there's such a thing as a natural gift for counseling, you had it, like no other person in the room."

As I listened to Ritsuko's story, I couldn't help but think how ridiculous it was. "You're making way too much of it. Using physical contact to calm someone was the first thing they taught us in the workshop. Everybody knew how to do it."

"No!" Ritsuko sounded almost indignant. "And this wasn't something I sensed from you all the time. Usually, you seemed emotionally closed off, if anything. But at that moment, when it really mattered, some incredible empathic power just descended upon you. I don't think I was the only one who felt that way, either. I think Professor Kunisada noticed it, too. I have no trouble understanding why he was drawn to you. He saw in you something he lacked, and he wanted it."

I couldn't suppress a smile. Too bad he wasn't listening.

But in all truth, though Ritsuko was telling me that I had more of a gift for psychotherapy than Kunisada, I'd quit the field out of despair at my own impotence and mental weakness. I had looked into the dark depths of my psyche and found there the desire to control other people, to take hold of their weaknesses to force them to follow me—I took pleasure in taming people and dominating them. I decided I'd be better off in a job that didn't involve people's minds. I'm too proud. Maybe I was a lot like Kunisada in that respect.

Ritsuko could see that I was at a loss for an answer, so she changed the subject. She was a quick woman.

"Anyway, what brings you back here today?"

Ouch. I didn't know what to say about that, either.

"Um, I came to see Professor Kunisada. There was something I needed to consult him about. I hadn't seen him in ten years."

"Really?" Her eyes opened wide, as if to say, *Do you expect me to believe that's all?* True, it didn't make much sense, logically. Anything I would possibly have to talk to Kunisada about would be psychological, and it was asking a lot to think that two ex-lovers could talk calmly about something like that, even ten years later. But Kunisada had judged himself capable, hadn't he? That was why he'd agreed to counsel me.

"Professor Kunisada's as self-confident as ever," I finally said.

Ritsuko hastened to add, "Oh, sorry, I didn't mean it like that."

Like what?

I needed to change the subject. "So what's your research about, Ritsuko? I seem to remember you were planning to specialize in cognitive psychology."

She gave a chagrined laugh, but her answer was cheerful enough. "You're not going to believe it, but I'm doing work on shamanism now. Sometimes I surprise even myself."

"Shamanism? You mean, like, witch doctors?"

"Hey, don't look at me like that. Not that I'm not used to it."

It was just that the Ritsuko Honda I knew was so sober and rational.

"I told you I did fieldwork in Okinawa, right? Well, I was on Miyako Island doing work on *yuta*, the local shamanesses. I was trying to understand the role they play in their communities."

"Wow. I'd never have pegged you as someone interested in the occult. You always seemed like a more cut-and-dry type of person to me."

She gave me a straightforward answer. "You're right. But maybe that's precisely why I was attracted to the spiritual, why I ended up diving right into it. That's how we're made: we seek balance. Something I couldn't naturally understand was exactly what I needed, I guess."

Maybe she was right. Clinical psychology proved to be too heavy for me. The dark study of how to make one's way into people's psyches was maybe too *like* me—I couldn't bear the double load. Maybe I'd chosen to work in the world of finance in order to gain some balance.

"So do shamans still exist?"

"Sure they do. In Japan there are the *yuta* of Okinawa, the *itako* in the Northeast, and the *fuchi* of the Ainu in Hokkaido. Not to mention in a lot more places around the world—Korea, China, Russia, Latin America, Australia, Europe too. But shamanism originated in Northeast Asia. It was only after they were discovered there that the study of shamans spread throughout the world. The history of shamanism goes way back, too. In Japan we've discovered what we think are the bones of a shaman from almost two thousand years ago. Not only that, but their numbers started to increase in the '90s. They're calling it the Age of Neo-Shamanism."

"Increasing? Shamans?"

She leaned her head as she thought for a moment. "Well, I suppose 'self-styled shamans' would be more like it."

"Hunh."

I'd heard that shamans were supposed to be able to summon the dead. I wondered if that was true. If it was, I wanted to be able to ask my brother why he'd died. I remembered, too, what Kunisada had told me: "To ask why your brother died is to enter the domain of religion, or the occult." Which might be true. But then again, what was so bad about relying on religion or the occult, anyway? They were just more tools human beings had developed to help them get by.

"So what role *do* shamans play in their communities?" I asked.

Tossing her empty Dasani bottle into a nearby trash can,

Ritsuko rose and said, "I guess you could think of them as a sort of electrical outlet for the whole community to plug into."

13

I went home and called Kimura.

It was only just past five in the evening, so he should've still been at work. But when I dialed his office number I got his answering machine. I tried his cell phone—the same. Incredulous, I tried his home number, and a very down-sounding Kimura answered. I'd been in a good mood for the first time in ages, but now I could feel it withering away.

"What's wrong? You don't sound like yourself."

Kimura's sounding depressed was no reason for me to start feeling bad, and yet I did. He mumbled something in reply.

"Hey," I said. "Want to go on a trip?"

"A trip?" He was obviously surprised.

"Yeah, to Okinawa. Miyako Island, actually. There's something I'd like to check out there. I'm still worried about your health, so I thought I'd see if you wanted to come along. It'll only take two or three days, and we can go whenever's best for you."

"To what do I owe this good fortune?"

"Nothing really. Just think of yourself as my photographer and bodyguard."

"You're in a good mood today, aren't you, Yuki?"

"Yeah, I guess I am."

But Kimura didn't seem to be. I found myself getting annoyed at him.

"So what'll it be? Are you in or out?"

There was only silence on the line for a while. Then, "Yuki, I have something to tell you. Hear me out, okay?" His voice was oddly gruff, as if what he had to say was difficult.

"What?"

"I went to see a doctor the other day. You seemed so worried about how I smelled that I thought I'd go just to set your mind at ease. I figured it was a good opportunity, so I went ahead and had a full check-up. And they found 'indications of cancer.' I have a tumor in my rectum. They're not sure yet if it's malignant or not. I'm going into the hospital tomorrow for tests. I don't know how long I'll be there. So, you see, I can't go to Okinawa with you. Sorry."

A chill shot up my spine.

"You're joking, right?"

"No, I'm not. Looks like your nose knows. Maybe you weren't hallucinating after all. I do have something wrong with me."

I could tell he was trying to sound light-hearted. But he was never any good at hiding his fears. What a fucking moron.

"I'm coming over," I said.

But his reply was firm. "Don't move, Yuki. I'm coming to your place."

The chills crawling up my spine were so bad it felt like the skin on my back was being peeled away. I'd smelled something on him. But I hadn't thought there was any hard evidence to link that smell to death. I certainly hadn't thought he had cancer.

I curled up on the floor. I couldn't wrap my mind around it. This kind of thing just didn't happen. Reality was crumbling around me.

As I lay there motionless, I could feel a pulse through the floor, like some bizarre heartbeat. I stroked the floor. Through my fingertips I could feel a subtle trembling. I thought I felt a faint electric current. What was happening?

Suddenly I saw Taka in my mind's eye.

I felt his presence. It couldn't be. But when I turned around, he was sitting there, only about a foot away from me. My dead brother was sitting right next to me, hugging his knees and staring off into space.

Night was coming. The whole room glowed red in the setting sun. It didn't seem real—it seemed like some kind of grotesque dream sunset. I inched backward, away from my brother. His face in profile looked sad. This was real. I could feel his breath. He was cradling a clock, the old clock I'd brought back from his apartment.

The clock's ticking was pulling me in. My consciousness concentrated itself on the ticking, there was nothing I could do to resist. My brain was picking up on some code hidden in the sound, which it converted into an image. I could perceive its outlines. I was a piece of equipment for converting the code into visuals. The image was the clock's memory. No, this wasn't reality. It was an illusion.

Yet the image had to be real: he was sitting there, clutching his knees to his chest like an idiot.

The doorbell rang. My brother disappeared, and all that was left was the clock.

Kimura stood at the door.

He seemed to be wrapped in some sort of thin membrane. He lacked reality. He *was* real, and yet he seemed as insubstantial as a dream.

"Are you all right, Yuki? You're pale."

He came in and put his arm around me. He held me close, and suddenly he was kissing me, putting his tongue into my mouth. It wasn't cold, but I couldn't stop shivering. What was wrong with me? I couldn't calm down. I was scared. I felt like I was about to be carried away somewhere, and I couldn't stay still.

"I feel like I'm about to break! Something's trying to come inside me. My dreams are running over."

He tried to calm me down, but the minute he hugged me tighter, it was like a switch flipped in my brain. I was overcome with an absolutely insane lust. I couldn't control it.

I pushed Kimura down and violently covered his lips with mine. I forced my tongue into his mouth and licked his gums. At first he was taken aback and tried to push me off, but I clung to his neck and grappled with him until he gave up and climbed on top of me. I tore open the buttons on his shirt and sank my teeth into his flesh. I wanted to rip him to shreds. I felt every synapse in my brain firing madly. I could see them, flashing irregularly. My breathing came forced, fast and shallow.

"Calm down, Yuki," he said, as he undid his belt, but I couldn't wait. I bit his arm. "Ouch!" he cried, and forced my head away with the palm of his hand. "Get a hold of yourself!" He held my head between his hands and blocked my mouth with his. His oral cavity was filled with the stench of my brother's corpse, but now, that smell filled me with nostalgia again, and I inhaled it deeply as I entwined my tongue with his.

"Suck on these," I said, ripping open my blouse and flipping up my bra. "Hurry!" Kimura did as he was told. He took hold of my breasts and started licking my nipples. "Harder, harder!" Not nearly good enough. "Squeeze them! Please! Harder!" His fingertips pressed a little stronger now. I could feel them burrowing into my breasts. I began to go into a daze. I wanted to forget everything. I would become completely empty. I was hollowed out and I craved something to fill me up.

I reached out and touched his penis. It wasn't hard enough yet. I crawled toward it and took it into my mouth, letting my tongue trace the veins that ran up and down its length. I poked the tip of my tongue into the little slit at the end over and over. I let my mind go and thought of nothing but sucking him. I concentrated my whole being on his slightly twitching penis. Then I let my tongue play over the area between his penis and his anus. Kimura started caressing my genitals with his tongue, lapping at my labia. The touch of his tongue ran up my backbone and shot out the top of my head. It felt unbelievably good. I stuck my finger in his anus and sucked on his penis, and it started to jump like waves were beating it. When I took it out of my mouth it looked like some ancient artifact, a small reddish-black version of the Moai on Easter Island, gazing heavenward, wet and gleaming from my saliva. Sticky fluid was oozing out from the tip. Driven by lust that was almost like an itch, I slowly straddled the Moai and inserted it into my vagina. I was like an outlet. I was connected to him now. But what for?

Kimura started moving his hips roughly. We were connected. What for? He stimulated my anus with his fingers as he worked his hips. I started to cry out. I liked the feeling of being kneaded and stirred like that. It was so good. My hips started to move of their own accord. *Oh, that feels good, more, more*, I breathed as I arched my back and moved my hips, ungraceful in my passion. *That feels good, really good. That's it, it's really happening, I'm coming back, this is my body.*

I have no shoes on. It's pathetic.

I'm in an unfamiliar town, in a shabby shopping arcade. There's nobody on the street, it's the middle of the day, and there I am, under the arcade roof, walking in just my socks. I'm hoping I don't run into anybody. If anyone sees me, they'll misunderstand. Misunderstand what? Well, they just wouldn't understand. But why am I walking around in such a strange place? Then again, it looks an awful lot like the shopping arcade in the town I was born and raised in. Ah, it's a dream. I'm dreaming again.

There's a shoe store. It looks like your typical small-town shoe store. A bunch of out-of-style shoes lined up randomly and artlessly in the storefront. I walk in, thinking to buy some shoes.

There doesn't seem to be anybody in the store. It's quiet. No signs of life here either.

I look carefully at the racks of shoes, but each and every pair is way out of date. And none of them are my size, either. They're all either too big or too small.

But I figure buying some would beat walking around in my socks, so I fish around in my pockets. I don't have enough money, only some change, not nearly enough to buy shoes. Oh, what the hell. There's nobody around. I might as well just take a pair. So without blinking, I proceed to steal like it was the most natural thing in the world. Not a pang of guilt. I'm shoplifting without a second thought.

The shoes I settle on are a little bit too small for me, but they're the best-looking ones I can find. I slip them on and start to hurry out of the store.

But the second I turn toward the door, I realize that the owner is there somewhere watching me. Oh, shit. I can feel him there, looking daggers at my back.

If I run, I'll just look more suspicious. I have to walk out like everything's normal. But my movements are jerky. The stolen shoes are tight and hard to walk in. I'm limping slightly.

"But I don't have any shoes," I woke up mumbling to myself.

"Hnnh? What?" Kimura was lying next to me, and he rolled over to face me. That's right, we fell asleep after having sex.

"Nothing. I just had a dream about shoplifting shoes because I didn't have any."

Kimura laughed. "Pathetic dream."

"Yeah." All my joints ached like I was waking up on the morning after running a marathon. I'd been so turned on, that was why my muscles had seized up. Why had I been so turned on?

"I'm thirsty. You want something to drink?"

"Yeah."

I got up, put on some pajamas lying nearby, and got some apple juice from the fridge. Articles of clothing were scattered everywhere on the living room floor. I poured juice into two cups and handed one to Kimura.

"Thanks." He gulped it down. "You know, Yuki, you scare me sometimes when we're doing it."

I laughed, "Why? Am I too rough for you?"

He shook his head. "You remind me of things."

"What things?"

"Things." He stared in silence at his empty cup. "What are you going to do in Okinawa?"

"I'm going to meet someone. There's someone there I really want to talk to."

"Who?"

"How can I explain it? She's kind of a medium...a shamaness."

"A shamaness? What business do you have with someone like that?"

"I'm not exactly sure yet myself, but I thought I might be able to find out what happened to my brother. Why he keeps appearing to me, whether he's just a hallucination or whether something has caused his consciousness to linger in this world. I need to know."

Kimura snorted. "I had no idea you were so into the occult. I only knew the Yuki obsessed with the stock market. I'm really seeing a different side of you lately. Don't get me wrong, it's interesting. Just kind of unexpected."

"It's not that big a deal."

"There's no such thing as ghosts. Take that odor you kept smelling. That turned out to be absolutely real. You said it yourself, didn't you? Sometimes shock can make people's sensory organs so sensitive they can detect things they usually can't. That's what's happened to you: your perceptions are heightened temporarily, and that's why so many things are bothering you. But once you calm down, things'll go back to the way they were."

"I'm not so sure."

"Well, I am."

"But what about what you told me? You said the first time we slept together I was staring at the ceiling and calling to my brother. But I didn't know he was dead yet. I only found out the next day, when I got home. Don't you think that's strange?"

"No, I don't. After all, you also told me that you had a feeling your brother was going to die. Subconsciously, you always expected him to die. So when you got drunk you had a hallucination."

I'd thought of that, too. But my take was a little different.

"Maybe that was an illusion. But I saw it. And I still see it. It doesn't matter if it was a hallucination; I saw it. It's real to me. I have to check it out, by whatever means necessary. If there's someone who might have a clue, I have to go talk to that someone, no matter who it is. I have to figure out why these things are happening—what's happening to me. Before it destroys me."

By the end I was crying. It must have been a deeper shock than I'd realized for me to be crying like this. I wasn't the type of girl who cried easily. I realized I must have been getting even more eccentric than I'd imagined. My self-restraint was going. I had to do something, quick. I was getting hysterical, neurotic.

"I'm sorry, Yuki. I was just trying to reassure you. I should have known that platitudes don't work on you. It's a habit, that's all. I'm a *ridiculously good guy*, see, so I always go and try to act nice. Sorry about that. You're right, this is your problem. You're the one who's suffering. I promised I'd help you, so I'd better not argue with you, huh? Thanks for inviting me along—sorry I can't go."

Cool it, I told myself, over and over. Kimura hasn't done anything wrong. You can't take it out on him. You can't hurt him.

"You and your apologies. I can go to Okinawa alone, I don't need you to come with me. A sick man would just be a hindrance. You have your tests tomorrow, right? Aw, I'm sure it's nothing to be worried about. Even if it's cancer, it can't kill you, can it? After all, this thing seems healthy enough!" I squeezed his crotch through the blanket. He laughed and hugged me.

"It could've been serious if I'd let it go, though. I really owe you, Yuki. Your nose is something else. You're like a K-9 dog. I'll let you know as soon as the results come back."

When he brought his face close, I smelled it again.

I was getting used to it by now. In fact, I felt pretty intimate with the odor. I'm sure that in the days of the hunter-gatherers, that's how everyone felt. Still, it seemed to me the smell was lying more heavily on Kimura now.

Maybe he was going to die, I thought, as I considered his face in profile.

14

"Are you familiar with the *Mondo Cane* movies?"

Kunisada shook his head.

"Well, there's this scene with a schizophrenic boy. He thinks he's a robot, and he can only move when he's connected to an outlet. My brother mentioned the movies to me several times before he died, for some reason. I think they must have left a deep impression on him. I rented them not long ago and watched them. And it struck me that maybe my brother was identifying with that schizophrenic boy."

"I see. He moved when...he was connected to an outlet." Whenever Kunisada started to analyze something, he sounded garrulous without realizing it. "As you say, your brother probably felt close to the boy—he empathized with the boy. There was something in his life that he felt he shared with the boy; your brother felt disconnected at key moments. When he was disconnected, he could no longer move his body. He became dysfunctional. He felt he was at the mercy of something not subject to his will."

"Do you mean he felt powerless in the face of fate?"

"Not so much fate as himself."

"Is that all?" I muttered. Kunisada darted a glance at me.

"Is there something else?"

"There was a vacuum cleaner in the room where my brother died. It was still outletted, as if he'd decided to do a little vacuuming, but there was no sign he'd actually gone through with it. It was as if when my brother connected the vacuum's plug, his own came out. When I first entered my brother's apartment after his death, that outlet caught my eye, and it's been bothering me ever since. Like that was his last message to me. I feel like there must be some deep meaning to it, something he was trying to tell me."

Kunisada waited a while, and then asked, "What do you associate with the word 'outlet'?"

I hesitated—how much should I tell him?

"What do I associate with it?"

"That's right. The real question is what 'outlet' means to *you*."

"Well, like I said, I think of it as a code, maybe related to my brother's death...."

"Your brother's gone. The dead don't speak. The one hung up on outlets now is you, Yuki."

I couldn't think of a response. I could only ask myself if he was right. Was my brother really gone? If so, what about what I'd seen?

"You wanted my opinion on your brother's death. Just this once, let me give it to you straight. This may be a harsh way of putting it, but I don't think the way your brother died was unusual in the least. We see this sort of thing every day— it's a clinical psychologist's bread and butter. The world is filled with people who have no definable malady, but who lack the strength to go on living. They die in ways that aren't quite suicide but aren't illnesses either. There are more of them every year. They just slip away, and hardly anybody notices. Usually the cause of death is put down as something vague like 'heart failure.' They're treated as normal illness-related fatalities. Your brother was one of them. His wasn't as rare a case as you seem to think. There are quite a few people who just stop eating until they die—I'd go so far as to say it's a fairly popular method. I'm sure it's not very kind of me to say this, but I'm just not that interested in your brother's death. I've already seen such cases. They add up to maybe one percent of the population, and I imagine they've probably always been around. They're not exactly mentally ill, so they don't attract our attention. They disappear and nobody ever inquires into the reasons. What can anybody do? Nobody can save them. Life is hard for such people; that's just the way it is for them. It's a personality thing. Of course there are all sorts of external factors as well, but the combinations are simply too varied to be analyzed effectively. When someone dies because he just couldn't live, it's nobody's fault. Maybe it's fate. I don't know. Nobody knows but the man himself. Your brother, Yuki, is dead. Therefore, the reason for his death will always remain a mystery. And you cannot solve that mystery. Of course, if you want to try, that's up to you, but you'll never find the answer you're looking for. Because, finally, you're *you*. You're not your brother. The problems you face are *your* problems, *your* doubts. Unless you realize this, and embrace it, you're in danger of losing yourself. Of course, sometimes we only find ourselves by losing ourselves."

I found it unpleasant to be told that starving oneself to death like my brother did was a popular way to go. It was humiliating to be informed that something one was obsessed with was utterly commonplace. But maybe it was. Maybe there were a lot of people like my brother in this world. There probably were.

"So you're saying, Professor, that my fascination with outlets is my own problem."

"In a word, yes. There's something within you that makes it advantageous for you to fixate upon outlets, and so you do."

"And because I'm fixated on outlets, I zeroed in on the plugged-in vacuum in my brother's apartment."

"Perhaps. I won't venture to guess. The point I want to get across is that, analytically speaking, it will be impossible for you to find out why your brother died. That's a job for spiritualists, or religionists. You're perfectly free to seek answers in other fields like that. But what you and I are endeavoring to do right now is to find, within *you*, the reason you're experiencing the smell of death. Don't forget that. Face yourself."

He made a show of looking at his watch, and then said, in his businesslike way, "Time's up. We'll meet again next week."

I couldn't find the ladies' room. Kunisada's counseling room was located in one of the new buildings, and I didn't know it like I did the older halls. I wandered around, down a flight of stairs and up a hall, until I finally found one and used it. It was a new, clean bathroom. It even had a noise-reduction system to save water. Otherwise, women tended to flush over and over to muffle the noise of their bodily functions.

When I bent over to wash my hands, I suddenly detected the faint smell of blood, mingled with aromatics. Shit.

At first, whenever I smelled rot it was always the stench of my brother's corpse, but lately I was able to make finer distinctions. This was the odor of blood. The odor of the tiles in my brother's apartment after they'd taken his body away. The smell of blood after it had jellied.

I wondered where it was coming from. I tried relying on my nose. I couldn't always smell things so distinctly—my circuits were interrupted until something happened to flip a breaker, and then I could perceive the smells. And once I became aware of them, I couldn't ignore them.

I opened the stalls one by one. There were four, and I sniffed each one but couldn't find the source of the smell. Looking around, my eyes fell on the door to the maintenance closet. I opened it. The odor was stronger there.

This is it, I thought. I brought my nose close to the various tools. The smell seemed to be coming from the mop. I picked it up. It was an old, ratty cloth mop, and the bottom of it seemed to me to be stained red.

Scared, I threw the mop back into the closet and shut the door.

I thrust my head into the sink and spat, trying to get the smell out of my mouth. *Something's definitely wrong with me. This isn't normal.* I raised my head and stared at my face in the mirror. I was white as a sheet. And there in the depths of the mirror I could see another figure.

Startled, I cried out. It was my brother.

I whirled around to see Taka standing in front of the door to the maintenance closet. He was no ghost, no illusion, nothing indefinite like that. He was standing there, looking just as alive as he ever had.

He had on the same dirty brown jacket he always wore. It was midsummer but he was dressed for winter. One hand was jammed in his trouser pocket, and the other had something thin and white dangling from it. A plug.

As I stood with my back to the sink, facing my brother's apparition, the world began to bend out of shape, bending under enormous pressure.

"Taka, what do you want to tell me?"

He didn't answer. He slowly offered me the plug.

"What about the plug? What are you trying to say?"

I yelled, but his expression didn't change. It had to be a hallucination after all. I closed my eyes, and when I opened them again he was gone.

I dashed down the stairs and out of the building. I cut across the lawn, shaggy with summer grass, and ran past the library. Suddenly, somebody grabbed my arm. Terrified, I shook off the hand.

"Yuki, what's wrong? Are you all right?"

It was Ritsuko. Seeing her, I felt immense relief. I hurriedly fixed my hair. I tried to put on a smile, but it didn't go very well. My fingers were trembling. She put an arm around my shoulders and sat me down on a nearby bench.

"I think you'd better rest a while. Maybe the heat's getting to you."

That must be it. I'm a little anemic, and so the heat must have been affecting me. My blood pressure was down, and I was in a haze. I nodded and clutched Ritsuko's hand.

"Do you want to talk about it?" Simple and to the point. "About this spiritual malady you're dealing with?"

We were sitting on a couch in a lounge in the library. It was almost closing time, and there was nobody around. As I gazed at Ritsuko's face, I recalled the dream I'd had about her, in which she'd scorned me. Why was she showing up in my dreams? And why had she leaked out of my dreams into reality?

"I had a dream about you not long ago, Ritsuko."

"Oh yeah?"

"A few days after the dream was when we ran into each other for the first time in years."

She seemed amused by this. "You're just the type to get premonitions like that, aren't you?"

"On the contrary, things like that never happen to me."

"I find that hard to believe. I've always seen a shamaness in you."

I had no idea what she meant. But she held some sort of key—why else would she have emerged from my dreams like this?

"I've been having hallucinations lately." I couldn't overcome the urge to tell her. "My older brother died about a month ago, and ever since then I've been seeing his ghost or whatever. The first time was right after I'd heard about his death, when I was on my way back to my parents' house. I was standing by an unmanned railroad crossing, and I saw him on the other side. My brother died under unusual circumstances. I guess you could call it a kind of suicide. He shut himself in his room and wasted away. Kunisada says a lot of people do that nowadays."

Ritsuko listened.

"Anyway, his corpse was in an awful condition when they found it. Because of the heat it had been decomposing and was smelling horrible. His blood had congealed on the floor and there were maggots crawling around in it. He was so far gone that at the funeral, the mourners all ended up vomiting because of the stench. And me—ever since I smelled that stench coming from my brother's corpse, I've been able to pick out the scent of human decay from among other smells. Now, that's strange, wouldn't you say? First visual hallucinations, and now olfactory ones. I'm afraid I'm way past neurotic and into schizophrenic."

I grew calmer as I explained. Everything decays when you put it into words. Maybe that decay was a blessing.

"You haven't told Kunisada about the hallucinations, have you?"

"No, I haven't. How did you guess?"

"Easy. You know if you told him, he'd treat you."

I found myself gaping at her. She was right. I didn't want

to be *treated*. I wasn't really sick. Of course, thinking I wasn't probably meant I was.

"So what was it just now? Another hallucination?"

That's right, Ritsuko had always been this frank. "Yes. I was in the ladies' room in the new building, and I smelled blood. It turned out to be coming from a mop in the maintenance closet. Of course, that doesn't mean anything. It's probably all in my head. But it seemed real to *me*. It's actual. I can't deny it. And then, when I looked in the mirror, I saw my dead brother's reflection. I spun around in shock, and there he was standing by the closet. He seemed very real, just like a living person. Only, when I called to him he didn't answer. He was holding a plug in his hand. When I blinked, he was gone."

"A plug?"

I nodded and reached into my bag for the snipped-off plug.

"Yuki, do you always carry one of these around with you?"

It was the vacuum cleaner plug that the guy from the cleaners had clipped off and given to me. I'd been carrying it around like a keepsake from a boyfriend.

With a look of distaste, Ritsuko picked up the white plug with two fingers.

"But this isn't an outlet, Yuki."

"Eh?" I squeaked. Ritsuko gave a wicked laugh.

"This is just a plug. What you're hung up on are outlets."

As I watched Ritsuko inch open the door to the maintenance closet, all my fears began to seem foolish. I felt like we were grade-schoolers on a dare.

She'd insisted that she wanted to smell the blood for herself, so I'd come back to the ladies' room with her. But for all her boldness earlier, now she looked kind of scared.

"This mop?"

"Yes."

I hadn't been imagining it. I could smell the blood again now. But it wasn't the smell of decomposition. It was more like the scent of *fresh* blood.

"I wouldn't have noticed it myself, but it does look like there's a blood stain. But I don't smell anything."

"Maybe somebody cut herself, and mopped up the blood with this."

"Maybe so. If we asked at the office, they might know."

She dropped the mop, slammed the door, and made a great show of wiping her hands clean.

"And then you saw your dead brother's reflection in this mirror?"

Now that she was cross-examining me, the whole incident began to feel unreal, like a daydream. "Right. I thought ghosts weren't supposed to be visible in mirrors, but I saw him. I turned around, and he was there. I must be going crazy. I'm sorry, Ritsuko, just forget the whole thing. Just put it down to my delusions."

"Not so fast." She raised her eyebrows, as if I'd said something ludicrous. "I can't forget something like that once I've heard it. Plus, Yuki, didn't you say that you dreamed about me? Do you think it was sheer chance that made us run into each other like this? No, it means something. I think you need my help. Don't you?" She seemed to have some specific plan in mind.

"I don't know. I don't even know you that well, Ritsuko."

She made an exaggeratedly sad face. "That's right. You were never interested in the likes of me. Well, like I said before, I was always interested in *you*. So I'm really glad we met again like this. I might even be able to help you out regarding what you want to know."

"What I want to know?"

She nodded portentously. "The meaning of outlets. That's what you want to know. Right?"

"Yes," I said, more emphatically than I meant to.

Ritsuko was looking at me gleefully. "There, that's the expression. There's this particular look you have whenever you're excited about something. Did you know?"

"Are you making fun of me now? Give me a break."

"I'm not making fun of you. I just want to see the real you."

I didn't understand what she meant. The real me?

"I'm absolutely positive. Yuki, you're a shamaness."

Laughing, she took my arm and we started walking.

We were moving at Ritsuko's pace. Maybe because of my confused psychological state, I had been swept up by her. Following her lead, we ended up pub-crawling through several establishments in a corner of Shinjuku I wasn't familiar with. Narrow backstreets filled to the gills with little bars, every one of them a dark, hushed hideaway. Ritsuko would walk right in as carefree as if it were her own house. We went to one place after another.

I just tagged along, in a fog. It was easier that way. I didn't feel like being alone. I thought that, if I was with somebody, then maybe I'd at least be able to stay in this world.

I had no idea how long we'd been barhopping—my sense of time was hopelessly vague. We were sitting at a table in the depths of a strange bar when I realized how drunk I was. Candlelight danced on stone walls. The low, domed ceiling was also made of stone. The place felt like a cave.

"Hello." The speaker, a woman, sat down at our table. Ritsuko addressed the woman as "Ako." Her makeup was thick, and it was dark, so I couldn't tell her age with certainty but she seemed to be about fifty. She wore rings on her fingers with big green and purple stones, and an unusual pendant around her neck. And a crystal bracelet, to boot. She was a walking mineral catalog. I felt something loud and discordant about her, something really out of whack.

"Ako, this is Yuki Asakura. Yuki, Ako owns this place."

I bowed.

"Yuki saw a ghost today."

Hearing this, the woman narrowed her eyes at me. "Well, now, is that so? I see. You've had somebody die on you, haven't you? That's who appeared to you. A man—perhaps an older brother?—thin, about forty, with a bad complexion…"

I was shocked. "How do you know that?"

Ritsuko was happy to answer for her. "Ako is psychic."

"Psychic?"

The old me would have laughed and then gotten up and walked out. But now, I wanted somebody to tell me what was happening to me and I didn't care who it was.

I said to her, "May I ask you something? How does this man appear to you? Can you see him? Or are you aware of him some other way?"

Ako twirled the whiskey-and-water in her glass. "Hmm. It's not exactly a visual image. Some people say they see images, but I find that rather frightening. It's not like that for me. It's more vague, more nuanced. It's like hearing a sound inaudible to others. I can pick up on those signals. I'm not sure myself how I do it, but I hear them. They tell me things. And based on what they tell me, I kind of patch together an image—but the image is just something I'm imagining on my own. It's like what you do when you're reading a book."

But it wasn't like that for me. It wasn't signals, I really saw the images.

"Are they what people call ghosts?" I asked.

Ako laughed, and it seemed like all her gems were chortling. "There's no such thing as ghosts. My, what a scary thought!"

"But you say you sense my brother through me—what do you call that?"

"I don't know. Perhaps simply a very strong thought. The human psyche is energy, after all."

So, because I was obsessed with my brother, she was able to "read" him through me?

"Hey, Ako, don't you sense something special about Yuki?"

Ako once again squinted at me. Or, rather, she stared at a point just behind me, as though to unfocus her eyes.

"I'm not sure. I don't feel anything. I don't see anything unusual. She seems very strong. Very logical—the impression I get is almost that of a man. How shall I put it? She puts up a firm guard. She's like a window with the blinds closed."

"Hmm...a firm guard, huh? Me, I think Yuki's very unusual."

I interrupted Ritsuko to ask Ako, "What is it about me you're reading? My heart? My thoughts? Something else entirely? This information you pick up on—what form does it take? Where does it exist?"

Ako gave an awkward smile. "My, we ask difficult questions, don't we? I don't know. Maybe it's your heart. People emit all sorts of signals invisible to the eye. People radiate them like fine particles. I think what I'm doing is catching the strongest particles and reading them. But I can only read a few of them. Most of the particles are too miniscule, and I can't make heads or tails of them. It's hard to express, but that's my impression of how it works."

"And what good does it do you to be able to read them?"

It was an honest question.

"Not a great deal. It's a nice parlor trick, especially if you run a bar."

"Well, what are the drawbacks?"

She gave it to me straight. "Chronic migraines, paranoia, anxiety disorder, night terrors—frankly, being a spiritualist is a pain in the ass."

When I looked at my watch in the restroom, it was already past one in the morning. I decided I'd better go home. I started fixing my appearance in the mirror when suddenly Ritsuko came in. As soon as she saw me she pulled me into the stall.

"What are you doing?"

She latched the door and whispered, "It's too early for you to be going home yet."

I watched as she leisurely lit a long, slim cigarette. She took a drag and then offered it to me. "Here, try it."

"I don't smoke."

She laughed. "Silly. This isn't tobacco."

The ladies' room was small, and it was already filled with a sweet fragrance.

"Is this marijuana?"

"You've never tried it?"

"No."

"Really?" She looked surprised. "I want to see the real you," she said, pushing the joint into my mouth. I turned my head away.

"Are you scared?"

Why was she provoking me? I glared at her face, just inches from my nose, and then slowly sucked some smoke into my lungs.

"Keep it in your lungs for a while—don't exhale," she said, and took another drag.

The next thing I knew, I was alone, wandering along a deserted alley.

It must have rained at some point, just a passing shower, because the asphalt gleamed. The air was damp and bracing when I inhaled. It was almost morning.

I came upon a small park. My body was tired, so I sat down on a fence that surrounded a planter box in the park. It was cold and wet with dew. I was tired, but I didn't feel bad.

I happened to glance up at the sky. Crimson clouds swirled overhead in a huge, languid vortex. It was almost as if they were sucking something up from the streets of Shinjuku. The clouds' center looked like a giant, blackish-red whirlpool of meat.

As I stared, flabbergasted, somebody spoke to me: "Can you see it, too?"

I turned toward the voice. A man stood there. His hair was cropped short and he wore a black shirt with raised collars. It was too dark to tell his age exactly, but he might have been in his thirties. He spoke Japanese with an accent, maybe Chinese.

I recoiled. His body smelled quite plainly of death.

"That vortex has been there for ten years," he said, as if to himself.

"What is it?"

"I'm not sure, but I think it's there for balance."

"Balance?"

He ambled over to me.

"Yes, that's right. It's preserving the world's balance. This town has too much mass. It's off-balance. That thing siphons off the excess energy and sends it somewhere else. It always appears before dawn, right around this time. It looks like it's made of flesh, doesn't it? It's sucking up energy and releasing it somewhere else."

"Where?"

He smirked. "How should I know? The Gobi Desert, maybe, or Siberia. Someplace like that, probably."

As I stared, I began to see fine reddish-violet particles being sucked up into the vortex. I realized they were the city's energy. They were a nasty color.

"You smell like a corpse. You really do. Like decomposing blood and dead bodies."

He sat down next to me and said, "Oh?" He didn't seem too surprised. I quickly realized where the smell was coming from: his shoes. The stench was rising from their soles, as if he'd been walking through a field of corpses.

"Your shoes stink."

He laughed pleasantly when I said this. "You're a funny girl." He ground out his cigarette on one of his soles. "I forgot to change shoes."

Then, without a word, he grabbed my arm and pulled me into a public toilet in a corner of the park. This place, too, was rife with the reek of putrefaction. Suddenly I had a wave of déjà vu. Something like this had happened to me before. I knew what was coming. I braced myself on the sink and stuck my rear out. Silently, he hiked up my skirt and pulled down my panties. He checked with a finger to make sure I was wet, and then entered me. I stuck my ass out farther for him. I realized I'd been wanting this to happen. He'd read me and complied.

"Sorry, but I'm in a hurry. I'll have to make this quick," he said, moving his hips. "But meeting you is a good omen. I think work's going to go pretty well today."

I could feel the walls of my vagina twitching as they sucked him in. I was bottomless; I could feel his energy burst out from between my eyebrows. I was a reddish-black vortex of flesh, sucking up his energy. The pleasure was incredible. His movements became more violent—he was slamming into me now, crying out with each thrust. I realized I was rubbing my own mound and moaning. This wasn't me; it was his memory. I didn't have sex like this. The man was screwing some other woman in his head. I was resonating with his memories.

With a strangely affected cry the man came. He pulled out, and his hot semen dribbled out of my vagina.

"Mine won't get you pregnant. Don't worry."

He put away his penis and washed his hands at the sink.

"You shouldn't hang around places like this. You're stoned, aren't you?"

Was I? I wasn't sure.

"I knew a woman like you in Shanghai once."

I figured that had to be who he was thinking of while he was doing it. It was she who played with her clitoris during sex. I wiped his sperm off my thighs with a tissue and pulled my panties back up. Just like a prostitute, I thought.

"What do you mean, a woman like me?"

He thought for a moment before he replied, "A woman connected to the Other Side."

15

"How are you feeling?"

An utterly predictable question. This was a kind of ritual, something that had to be done the same way every time, no matter what.

"Awful. The confusion seems to be getting worse," I said, slumping in the chair.

"When you say it's getting worse, what exactly do you mean?"

The air conditioning in the counseling room was too effective. I could feel my sweat rapidly cooling. I felt even more tired than before.

"I had a panic attack right after last week's session. I couldn't restrain my emotions. I became agitated." Even as I spoke I was getting frustrated with Kunisada's professional tone. I could feel my blood pressure rising.

"Do you remember anything from your episode of agitation?"

"I do. Even when I'm excited like that, there's always some part of my brain that's calm."

"In other words, you're conscious that you're abnormally excited?"

"That's right. That's what makes it so scary. And, in that partially calm state, I saw my brother." The words had a momentum of their own, and I just blurted them out. Shocked that I'd said it, I clamped my mouth shut. Too late. There was no way Kunisada would overlook this.

"You saw your brother? Where was this?" His tone had changed. He was attentive now, like an animal with some prey in sight. I could only resign myself.

"In the ladies' room downstairs. I happened to look up, and when I did, he was standing behind me. It was a very clear vision, indistinguishable from reality. He didn't disappear even when I spoke to him. It didn't seem like a hallucination—it was the real thing."

"Is this the first time you've hallucinated about your brother?"

I hesitated, but decided it wouldn't do any good to lie. "No. It's the third."

"You never mentioned it before."

"I couldn't."

"Why?"

"Well, if I told you I'd been seeing things on top of the smells, you'd conclude I'm sick."

"You don't know that."

"But I do. I was your student. Visual and olfactory hallucinations are early symptoms of delusionary schizophrenia. It requires specialized treatment including the administration of drugs."

Kunisada sighed and tried a counterargument. "You're not

me, so I'd appreciate it if you didn't try to make my decisions for me. Are you able to talk about the first and second hallucinations?"

I didn't want to. But if I refused I'd come across even more insane.

"The first time was when I was on my way back to my parents' after hearing the news of his death. I saw him standing near an unmanned railroad crossing in our old neighborhood that night. It only lasted a moment. The next time was in my room, and I was in an agitated state, and the third time was after our session last week…I could see him so clearly. It was as if he were still alive."

"He seems to be taking shape more distinctly each time."

"That's what it seems like. It's gotten so I can't ignore it anymore. I'm getting even more sensitive to the smell, too. I pick up the odor of death everywhere now, from gutters, from public restrooms in parks…. Professor, it's like the world is filled with rotting corpses."

I realized I was being quite reckless. I was fessing up out of desperation, leaning back in my chair with my head turned to the side. I couldn't look at him.

"Are you sleeping nights?"

"Yes."

"Well, then. If you were to need medicine, we'd have to go through the university hospital. What do you think? Do you need tranquilizers?"

"I'll leave that up to you. I'm no longer confident that I'm well."

"You're perfectly normal. It helps that you're being such a rational patient. People see all sorts of things. I'm not going to decide someone's ill just because they've seen a dead person. After all, we haven't been able to explain for certain why people dream."

His words relaxed me a little.

"Do your visions of your brother cause you to feel terror?"

"Not...really. I don't scream when I see him, or anything."

"You've accepted his existence, then?"

"I guess so. I mean, he was sort of like a ghost to begin with. He hasn't changed all that much." My words only struck me as strange after I had said them. I laughed. Maybe I didn't really think he was dead. Maybe if the undertaker had let me see his body, I wouldn't be having these problems.

"Today I'd like to ask you a little about your relationship with your brother. Would that be all right?"

"Yes."

"First I'd like you to go over the emotional circumstances of your assuming responsibility for your brother."

"As I told you before, he had become more and more violent toward our parents, and I wanted to get him away from Mom and Dad one way or another. I thought it was only a matter of time before they all murdered each other. But my brother didn't have anywhere else to go, and he was in no shape to get a job. So I had no alternative but to bring him home with me."

"How did he manage to come all the way to your place, if

he was in such a state?"

"I enticed him. I did everything I could to convince him. I told him I wanted to save him. I said, 'This is your last chance, so let's make a go of it, just the two of us.' My brother was a coward, and I was afraid he could tell if I was lying—there was nothing he feared more than being seduced and abandoned. So I threw myself body and soul into the effort—and in fact, I wasn't lying. I not only wanted to save him, I really thought I could. It was because he truly believed me that he was able to crawl out of his sealed room—out of the womb, if you will."

"Go on."

"I took care of him like a lover. I knew that would make him happy, at least temporarily. Pouring erotic energy into him was what was going to have the most immediate effect. I mean, counseling's like that, too, right? Lots of patients get well thanks to the transference they go through with their therapist. So I unconsciously became his 'lover.' My own brother's lover. But I think that for a little while at least he experienced some satisfaction. He was receiving absolute support and love from a female."

"Such a state couldn't continue forever, though—I'm sure you realized that?"

"I did, but I put it out of my mind. I knew things would break down eventually, but I thought I was buying time. I always intended to get him professional counseling once he'd gotten back some mental strength. I thought I could persuade him to receive proper treatment."

"Were you able to?"

"No, I wasn't. I'd miscalculated. I didn't think he'd be so stubborn about refusing treatment. He didn't want to see anybody other than me. Even if he had, he wouldn't have accepted them. I suggested once that he attend a support group for adult children of alcoholics, and he turned red with anger. I'm not nuts, he said. But... He moved in with me at the end of October, and by December he'd made quite a bit of progress. He was able to help with my work—typing things out on the word-processor, transcribing tapes, et cetera. So I thought I'd experiment with drawing him out of my room. I invited him to escort me on different occasions: to a friend of mine's pottery workshop, on a group hike, that kind of thing. If I brought him along, he'd come, but he wouldn't mingle with anybody. It wasn't that he was refusing to, he was just very nervous. My brother was defensive, and he was proud—he was just a mess of complexes. He was pathetically self-conscious, really easily offended, and I got tired just being around him. But that was nothing compared to how worn out he'd get from being around other people. The next day he wouldn't even be able to get out of bed. After a while he stopped taking me up on my offers."

It was painful to think about him trying to deal with other people. I could see him, dressed like a vagrant as always, delivering his caustic comments on politics or the economy: cynical, smug pronouncements that alienated everybody. He didn't care. This was the other side of his self-consciousness. He was so raw it hurt to watch.

"What kind of life did your brother lead in your apartment?"

"I gave him an allowance based on the work he did for me. I persuaded him to accept the arrangement by telling him that I needed his assistance. We agreed to a contract that he'd work a certain number of hours. I was very clear and above-board about money."

"I think that was exactly the right thing to do." Kunisada nodded, impressed.

My brother's lifestyle was quite austere, but still I had a hard time supporting him. For the first time I realized how hard it was to have another human be your dependent. It costs money for people just to be alive, to breathe.

"What did your brother have to say about finding a real job?"

"He said he wanted to, but couldn't, that he was sick. And it was true, he was in terrible shape. All those years of irregular eating had really done a number on his insides. He vomited a lot. But he kept eating junk food. It was almost like he was trying to destroy his health. Like he didn't want to get better. I think he wished he could just go on helping me like that, but I had no intention of allowing that to happen. In that sense, I think I betrayed him. After a while, I began to get disgusted with him. I was reaching my limit. I couldn't be around him anymore without feeling oppressed. Talking with him, he just sounded so irresponsible and selfish that I wanted to throw up myself. No matter how hard I tried to listen, I just couldn't— it made me sick."

"What kinds of things would he talk about?"

"The past. He only ever talked about the past. One long, incoherent string of memories. He'd berate Mom and Dad irrationally. It was painful to hear, he was so self-centered the way he'd complain about them. At first I tried hard to lend him an ear, because I knew that just listening to him was the best thing I could do to help him heal. But it got harder and harder to take. Having to hear him out was starting to make me ill."

"I understand. Since he was your brother, it was impossible for you to remain neutral."

That was it. The people he was cursing were my flesh and blood. My father and mother were a part of me. My brother never realized that when he was cursing them, he was cursing a part of me too.

"So I...I started to stay over at the apartments of male friends instead of coming home. At first I'd only stay away once or twice a week, but it gradually got worse and by April I was only coming home about once a week. I asked my brother to be responsible for the phone and the mail, and I'd give him work to do, computing my tax returns and attaching receipts. He did whatever I told him, although it took forever and he did it badly. He was doing his best, though, and I felt so sorry for him that it hurt. But I ended up distancing myself even further. I think he basically spent the whole month of May living alone in my apartment. When I happened to come home, I could tell he'd been polishing his word-processing skills, or reading every book I had in the place. I thought he was enjoying himself, after his own fashion. I wanted to believe that—I tried to make myself believe it. I mean, he didn't have to pay rent, and I gave him enough spending money. And then, on the fifth of June, I suddenly remembered it was my brother's birthday. I made up my mind to go home that day to help him celebrate, but I ended up accepting an invitation from a guy and went out drinking instead. I never made it home that night. When I finally got home two days later, my brother was gone."

And I'd been utterly relieved to find that my brother and his things had vanished.

"And then his body was discovered on the first of August?"

"Yes."

"You told me that you hadn't cried since your brother's death."

"I haven't shed a tear for him."

"Why do you think that is?"

"I don't know. Maybe because I never understood him. He was so irrational, so selfish, that maybe I feel anger toward him."

"And how do you think he felt about you?"

"I think he held a grudge against me. I think he felt I betrayed him."

"Do you really think that? Is that all?"

I was sure he thought, *See, you too betrayed me*.

"I think that he trusted me and relied on me, and when I ran away from him, he despaired. That's why he unplugged himself. From life. He quit living and starved to death."

I had seduced him and then ditched him—I knew that better than anybody.

"Do you think he really resented you? Do you think that's all he felt? Isn't it true that everything he did, he did for the family? Wasn't he living just as your family wanted him to?"

I was taken aback. "Just as we wanted him to? No way. He always did the opposite of what we wanted."

"No, that's not true. In every instance, he fulfilled his family's expectations exactly. Even if it hurt him. That's how he lived all along, don't you think? When he was a child, he could tell what your mother secretly wanted him to do, and he did it. If she wanted him to be a good boy, a nice boy, and not cause any trouble, he would do his best to act that way. Now, are you with me? The problem is this. He did his best. Of course, the results might have been completely different from what your mother had desired. But he had tried to oblige her to the best of his abilities. And his efforts needed to be rewarded with affection."

"Rewarded?"

"Yes. But the reward was too steep, as it were—nobody could offer it. Your brother was like an emotional loan shark. He'd force the family to be indebted to him, and then he'd try to collect at interest rates so high that the family would balk. He could never collect. That's why he resented his parents."

My brother had always told my mother, *It's your fault I'm like this.*

"There may have been something like that going on."

"He did the same thing to you."

"To me?"

"Yes. Somewhere deep inside your heart, you wanted him to just disappear, didn't you?"

Maybe so. Maybe I'd wanted him gone all along.

"Your brother read your desire and fulfilled it. He disappeared. That's all there is to it. He knew that the family wanted him to disappear—to work and be independent—and he responded, albeit imperfectly. He left you, rented an apartment of his own, and started a life of his own. It was the result of him swallowing all of his family's demands, after his own fashion. He was trying his best. I'm sure he didn't realize it would kill him."

"Are you sure about that?"

"Of course, no one knows but your brother. However, I suspect that at the moment he leased the apartment, he was satisfied that he'd complied with his family's demands one hundred percent. He didn't think he'd failed. Rather, I imagine he was thinking he deserved a reward for all his efforts. As a result, when his situation began to deteriorate, maybe he decided he no longer cared whether he lived or died."

"He's mad at me."

"Why do you think that?"

"Because I didn't pay him interest on his efforts. Maybe he's come back as a ghost to collect."

Kunisada glared at me. "Do you really believe that?"

"I don't know. I can't penetrate my brother's feelings. Every time I try it's like I run into a dull gray wall."

"To know your brother's true feelings would inconvenience you."

I didn't like the way he said it. How irritating. *Inconvenience?*

"You said it yourself, Professor: he's dead. Nobody can know his true feelings now."

"Why are you angry right now?"

I snapped back, "I'm not angry!"

"Ten years ago you underwent educational analysis with me. Do you remember what you said to me in our first interview?"

I drew a blank. "No, I don't." What could I have said that Kunisada would bring up now?

"You said you hated emotions." He gave a professional laugh and looked at his watch. "It's time. Let's stop here for today."

It wasn't fair to cut me off like that, I felt. It was extremely unpleasant. I wanted to say more, but I couldn't get my thoughts together. I stood up noisily and grabbed my bag. I was in too bad a mood even to say goodbye, so I just stomped to the door and opened it.

"Oh, that's right," Kunisada said behind me, as if talking to himself. "Do you remember Yamagishi? He was one of your classmates."

When I turned around, Kunisada was standing at the window with his back to me, peering through the blinds.

"He said something interesting at a staff meeting yesterday. Evidently one of his patients speaks of going into a trance as 'coming unplugged.'"

Yamagishi...It didn't ring any bells. Maybe I'd known somebody by that name.

"Yamagishi went on to med school here. He's in the psychiatry department at the university hospital now. He's an interesting fellow—he specializes in dissociative disorders. I'm sure he remembers you."

I bowed and slammed the door.

16

"Hey, do you remember Yamagishi?" I asked.

The heat of midsummer had lingered on well into September. Ritsuko and I were mopping sweat off our brows as we walked beneath the sycamores. The screeching of cicadas shook my eardrums.

"Yamagishi? You mean Mineo?"

It was so hot that we had to take refuge inside a coffee shop in the station. Only after I'd taken a big gulp of iced coffee was I able to relax. Ritsuko had said she was hungry, and she was eating a hot dog.

"The one working at the university hospital."

She nodded. "That'd be him. He's an interesting guy. Really well-versed in transpersonal studies. I've gotten into several debates with him over the psychological makeup of shamans. Oh, and—ten years ago, Yamagishi was one of your secret admirers."

"Bullshit."

"Why do you bring him up?"

"There's something I'd like to ask him."

"First Kunisada and now Yamagishi, not to mention the address of a shamaness. Psychologists, psychiatrists, gods—

you're mobilizing everybody, aren't you?" She reached into her bag and pulled out an envelope. "Here's what you asked for: the address of a *yuta* on Miyako Island. Her name is Miyo Kamichi. I think she'll see you if you mention me, but then again she might not. With these people, if the gods say 'no,' you're out of luck."

I took the envelope and thanked her, and then asked, "Do you remember telling me the other day that shamans function like electrical outlets for their communities?"

"Yeah, I guess."

"You also told me you knew about outlets."

She slowly swallowed a bite of the hot dog before replying. "Shamans are like the holes in the wall where electricity comes through, if that's what you mean. But instead of conducting electricity, they're connected to the unseen world. When people visit shamans, it's like they're plugging themselves into an outlet. In so doing, they connect to the world of the gods."

"Okay."

"Outlets and plugs are useless without each other. But together they complete a circuit—a circle, if you will."

My brother had been holding a plug, of course—not an outlet. Which meant...was he searching for an outlet to plug into?

"You need an outlet if you're going to use electricity, right? It's essential for supplying power. What happens with a shaman or a shamaness is that people who have exhausted all their life energy come to them to have it replenished. It used to be that communities had lots of life-energy supply points. 'Man shall not live by bread alone,' and all that. People need metaphysical energy to go on living."

"Metaphysical energy?"

"Maybe that wasn't the right way to put it. 'Metaphysical' sounds kind of unreal. 'Spiritual energy' might be more like it."

"Is this like what the Chinese call *chi*?"

"Actually we don't know exactly what it is. It hasn't been explained away. But an increasing number of people are coming to feel that we're alive due to some sort of life-energy. Recently the WHO added 'spiritual health' to its definition of a healthy person. Spiritual well-being is now recognized worldwide as a necessary precondition of physical health."

Then she asked, point-blank: "So why are you so stuck on outlets?"

I laughed. "I'm just playing with riddles. I've really no idea why I'm so hung up on them, but I am."

"Are you picking up on a wavelength?"

"What are you talking about?"

Ritsuko laughed. She had a laugh like a kingfisher. "You really don't know much about the spiritual realm, do you, Yuki? What I mean is, maybe you're channeling something outside your own consciousness. Something somewhere is transmitting, as it were, the word 'outlet,' and you're picking it up."

I was really beginning to feel like Ritsuko was dragging me into something. I sighed. "You're pretty infatuated with this occult stuff, aren't you? I mean, the other night you dragged me into that bar and all—you shocked me!"

She laughed it off. "*You* were shocked? Yuki, I turned my back for a minute and you disappeared! *That* was a shock. You know, you're really hard to read—I never know quite what you're going to do. What did you end up doing after that anyway? I'd gotten some really good stuff just for you, but it didn't seem to have any effect at all. Such a shame."

So was it a regular thing for her? "I don't really remember. Next thing I knew I was home waking up. Listen, don't pull anything like that on me again, okay?" I remembered the strange man, the one whose shoes smelled like corpses. Had that actually happened, or had it been a hallucination? I couldn't tell.

"Oh, that reminds me. The mop in the ladies' room. About a month ago, it turns out, a student suddenly lost a lot of blood in there, and they'd cleaned it up with that mop. Your nose is amazing, Yuki—maybe you were a police dog in a past life."

"Is that true? A lot of blood?"

"She had a miscarriage in there."

I really did have an abnormal sense of smell. Something was happening to my brain—but what? "All your talk about 'wavelengths' and 'transmissions'—it makes me sound schizophrenic." Then I laughed. Objectively speaking, my symptoms were indeed those of schizophrenia, "wavelengths" or no.

"Well, I think you should have a long talk with Mineo

Yamagishi about that. That's his specialty. They say he's turned into an excellent psychiatrist. I guess it's natural that someone as out there as Mineo would be good at understanding the ones who're way out there. It's a thin line, as they say."

"What do you mean—is there something wrong with him?"

"How should I put it? He might be a kind of shaman himself. A very intellectual, self-controlled modern shaman. You know, the word *shaman* comes from the Tungusic language of Siberia—it's what they used to call a person in a state of extreme excitement. But getting agitated and forgetting yourself in order to do your work is old-fashioned shamanism. These days shamans are much more rational and logical. Now that I think about it, Yamagishi is a lot like you, Yuki."

"Like me how? You mean I'm out there, too?"

"Well, you're on a different vector, but…in a way." She grinned and added, "You should meet him. I think he's at least got more style than Kunisada."

Mineo Yamagishi told me to meet him in the hospital waiting room in the middle of the night. "I can probably spare some time if you can come while I'm on duty," he said over the phone, sounding none too excited.

So at eleven that night I was sitting in the dim waiting room in the university hospital when I saw a tall, slim figure come walking down the hallway under the red emergency lights. He had on a white lab coat and looked listless. I stood and bowed, and he beckoned me with a curt, "This way." I remembered him now: the nasal Kansai accent, the crew cut, the wire-rimmed glasses. He hadn't changed much after all these years.

"It's kind of messy, but there's nobody in the office but me right now." The room we entered was pretty cluttered. He dusted off somebody's swivel chair and offered it to me. Then he tossed me a lukewarm can of coffee, saying it was all he had.

"Professor Kunisada told you about me?"

I gave a vague response. He shot me a derisive look. It was the first time our eyes had met. He hadn't even said a proper greeting, even though we were encountering each other for the first time in a decade. He was speaking to me as if we'd just parted yesterday.

"So why are you seeing that old fart anyway?"

I sighed. It was going to take guts to explain this. "Let's just say it's probably what you imagine."

He let out an obscene laugh. "You're playing counselor again. You never tired of it, did you?"

An unpleasant man. "I didn't come here to be subjected to your sarcasm. I have my reasons. I'm going to explain them now, and if you don't feel like helping me, just say so, and I'll get out of your way. Is that all right?"

That shut him up.

"I want to ask you about outlets."

He shrugged his shoulders.

"My brother died in August. He wasted away. A kind of slow-motion suicide, you might call it. He was always emotionally weak, but he wasn't mentally ill. And that was the problem. He was normal in a way that was extremely close to being abnormal. If you were going to give it a name, you'd probably say he had a personality disorder, or showed symptoms typical of children of alcoholics, or was a borderline case of something, maybe depression. Anyway, he starved to death. Before dying, he talked to me about outlets. He told me about a schizophrenic boy who wouldn't move if he wasn't plugged in. My brother seemed almost obsessed with the boy. I want to know why, and also why he wasted himself away like that, alone in his room like one of those old Buddhist monks who tried to become mummies."

Yamagishi was sitting backwards in his chair, with his chin on the edge of the backrest. He listened with his head down and his eyes pointed up toward me, perfectly still, as if he were searching his internal hard drive. Something had switched on inside him.

"How old was your brother?"

"Forty."

"When did he start to act funny?"

"It's impossible to pinpoint, but probably junior high. That's about when the violence started in the house. After that he got worse, but not steadily. He'd stabilize for a while, then deteriorate some more. About three years ago, though, he stopped going out, sleeping all day in his room and only waking up at night. He got more and more mentally unstable, lethargic—the usual pattern."

"Were his thought processes rational?"

"I think they were, right up to the end. No hallucinations, no voices—at least, not that I know of. But sometimes he'd sort of go into a daze. At first I thought he was about to have a seizure."

"Seizure?" Yamagishi froze. Was this guy a cyborg?

"Sometimes it was like his gaze was just floating in space. But he never lost consciousness. It was like his mind was onto something totally different."

"Epilepsy, maybe," Yamagishi muttered. "What was your brother interested in?"

"Interested in?"

"What kind of music did he like? What kind of books?"

"After he died we found a CD Walkman in his apartment. It had a Mozart disc in it. But he mostly liked jazz. His tastes in movies and literature were a bit unusual. He had all of Luis Buñuel's movies on video, and he liked Latin American novels—magical realism. He loved García Marquez's *One Hundred Years of Solitude*."

He often had *One Hundred Years of Solitude* lying on the table. When he'd moved in, he'd been happy to discover a copy in my bookcase. *You like this, too? I guess you are my sister*, he'd said.

"Maybe he was in a self-induced trance." Yamagishi spun his chair around.

"What do you mean?"

"It's not very widely known, but there are a lot of people with that sickness. We usually think of a trance as a drug-induced state, complete with hyperventilation. But it turns out that there are some people who can enter the state voluntarily. I bet your brother was like that."

"Would you mind telling me more about that?" I leaned forward.

"These people with their trances, they can take themselves in and out of their bodies at will. A lot of them are pretty daydreamy to begin with. At first they're just playing in their own fantasy land. Like kids, they'll get caught up in a state of make-believe, treating it as though it were the real world. Of course, they know they're just pretending. Lots of people like to daydream—there's nothing unusual about that. As grown-ups in the real world, these people encounter stressful situations. A lot of things in life don't go the way they'd like them to. And when these people get stressed, they take temporary refuge in daydreams. It's a self-defense mechanism. But as they keep running away from reality like that, one day, *bam*, they slip into a trance. They're beyond themselves. It's an incredible feeling, apparently. Once you experience it, you never want to get back to the real world again. Of course, they can't live their whole lives in a dream world—life goes on—so they try their best to live a normal life. But it's extremely hard, painful even, for these people to live by society's rules. So they slip into their trances. Think about it—what could me more convenient, more pleasant, than being able to slip into a trance like that all on your own, without the help of alcohol or drugs? It's not something just anyone can do. It's a talent. And when these people realize they have the talent, they start to cultivate it. They start experimenting with the best way to bring on the trances, training themselves—like modern versions of the old Taoist hermits, you know, with their magical powers. I bet that's what your brother was doing for those three years he closed himself off, shut up in his room. I bet he was training himself, day after day, trying to perfect his ability to slip into a trance at will. After all, he had nothing but free time, so he could spend all day practicing. I mean, it's not an easy thing to do— he probably kept thinking, *This time I'll get it, this'll be the one*, trying various techniques. Training."

I found the word *training* oddly persuasive. Watching my brother, I'd sometimes thought he looked like some sort of ascetic.

"So you're saying it's like escapism?"

His response was immediate. "No, not at all. There's none of the guilt you have with escapism. No feelings of guilt at all. In fact, he probably had a sense of superiority, a sense that he was experiencing a world other people couldn't."

To be sure, even in the midst of his dissolution, I always had the suspicion that my brother was somehow looking down on me. Maybe he was getting glimpses of an egoless world that I had no inkling of.

"It's not too different in essence from what some of those new religions teach, with their 'emancipation from worldly desires.'"

"*That's* what happens when you're emancipated?"

"Well, it all depends on the person."

I guess he was right. "What exactly is this trance state?"

"I imagine it varies from person to person. One of my patients says he leaves his body and hovers in the air about six inches in front of his face. He says he feels weightless. It's a really pleasant feeling, according to him. And it just so happens that the term these people use for slipping into their trance is 'pulling the plug.' What do you think of that?"

"And they can enter this state whenever they like?"

"I did have a patient like that. I asked him if he could pull the plug while I watched, and he said, 'Sure, I'll do it right now.' And when he'd done it, he actually did look like somebody whose soul had slipped out. 'Where are you now?' I asked. 'I'm outside my body, right in front of you, Doctor,' he said. 'Well, that's enough of that, now how about plugging yourself back in?' I said, and he came back. He was exhausted, and said it takes a lot out of him to plug in and come back again. Being in a trance doesn't mean they completely lose consciousness. He could still hear me. But they say that the more they do it, the deeper the trance gets, so that eventually they can shut out everything. They say it's kind of scary."

"Is it more painful for them to be plugged in, I mean, to be in the state where energy can flow into them? I can sort of understand that. Then again maybe I don't." I was having trouble organizing my thoughts.

"That boy you told me about—that's from *Mondo Cane*, right?"

This startled me. "You know it?"

He shrugged and laughed. "The little boy in that movie might have been happier unplugged, even if nobody on the staff at that hospital thought so. In cases like his, being unplugged is like having the boundaries between themselves and the world dissolve. They're insulated from physical stimuli—they're just souls in a state of altered consciousness. These people are overly sensitive to the world anyway, and it's much more comfortable for them not to be plugged into the world. When they're in that state they're not of this world. When their spirits are off gallivanting around without their bodies, they're like ghosts. If they do it for too long, they'll die. But since they like the other world better than this one, what can we say? They're making a choice based on personal preference."

So, different people define happiness in different ways.

"So do you think my brother just went to the Other Side for good?"

"I don't know. Nobody knows. Maybe he was just experimenting with trances, leaving and reentering his body, and he got better and better at it until he could do so at will. Then he was doing it all the time, and finally he couldn't come back anymore and just died. Not a bad way to go, if you ask me."

Maybe not. Yamagishi's explanation rang true. I could easily envision my brother slipping in and out of his body. He seemed the sort, proud to be going back and forth between the real world and another world only he knew about. He would have been contemptuous of the uncomprehending and their insistence that their reality was happier and more respectable. *There are two worlds. Why can't they understand that? Why do I have to live in their harsh world?*

"What came to him through the outlet?"

"Alien substances." He laughed softly.

"Huh?"

"The human mind obtains energy by absorbing and consuming alien substances. It's a system just like the body. It takes in all kinds of foreign objects and uses them to generate power. External stimuli, that's what I'm talking about. The data collected by our five senses are all foreign."

"And, unplugging stops the intake of alien substances?"

"Yup. It's a means of voluntarily shutting out stimuli. When there's no stimulus, the boundary between self and exterior disappears, and you feel one with the world. Seen from the outside it looks almost like autism, but to the person experiencing it, it's a perfect union with an internal universe."

I was taken aback. I'd always imagined a sense of oneness with the universe to be a more open kind of thing. "Is that what astronauts and people who've had near-death experiences are referring to?"

"No, the opposite, as far as astronauts go. The feeling of merging with the world that they describe is a kind of electric shock, you might say, more like receiving direct stimulus through a really powerful outlet. What I'm talking about occurs when the plug is pulled. It's a purely internal merging with the world. It's more social to be plugged in, but it's not like one's better than the other. Like I said, it's a kind of talent to be able to pull the plug. Not many people realize that, but then again not many people can do it."

My brother had intentionally blocked off all external

stimuli. He'd shut himself in his room, closed the shutters, and finally he'd pulled his plug.

"You've been a big help. Your explanation's more plausible than anything else I've heard so far. I'm glad I came to you. Thank you."

"Don't mention it," he said with a bashful smile. "Glad to be of service."

I looked at my watch. It was already two in the morning. "I'd better be leaving. Sorry to have kept you sitting here all this time."

We stood, and then Yamagishi stepped over and grabbed my arm. He pulled me toward him and whispered in my ear, "Hey, let's go to a love hotel."

Shocked, I stared back at him. He said nothing else, just kissed me lightly. His lips were dry, thin, and cold, but they felt good on mine. I didn't feel any revulsion. It wouldn't be a bad thing to spend a while longer with this guy.

"Don't you have to stay here?"

"My partner'll be back from his date soon. We'll switch."

Before he even finished saying this, the door opened and a young doctor hurried in. Sure enough, he smelled of soap.

17

Sex with Yamagishi was plain. Bland.

And that surprised me. The way he'd come on to me, I'd expected him to be more interested, frankly. But he did it almost as if it was a chore. We took showers, got into bed, kissed, and stroked each other, then he entered me. He did everything calmly and patiently. Having his fine, taut skin against mine gave me a kind of clean feeling. He didn't perspire, and he didn't smell at all. His body was cool the whole time.

I told him I wanted to lie on his arm. He laughed. I'm tired, I said, and he said okay. I buried my face in his armpit, but there was still no odor. It was a relief. I'd had enough of smells. Cradled on his arm like that I dozed off. When I woke up at dawn, Yamagishi was staring at the ceiling. His hard drive was clicking, I figured. Maybe he had the ability to slip into a trance himself. I rolled over and put my arm across his chest.

He spoke, sounding very earnest. "Yuki, why did you respond so enthusiastically?"

I lifted my head. "What do you mean?"

Our lips were close.

"I mean, it can't be such a fantastic thing to sleep with

someone like me. It's not like you're all that crazy about me."

I couldn't help but laugh. "Did I seem *that* into it?"

"You seemed overjoyed. I don't know, it actually made me kind of sad when we were doing it. Made me wonder what your story was." He said it bashfully, and without cruelty.

"I don't know what other women are like during sex."

"Oh. So no other man has said anything about it to you?"

"No."

"Well, then, let me be the first. You're really good, Yuki. The kind of woman who, if you sleep with a guy once, he'll always come back for more."

"Uh-huh, thanks."

"I mean, you make a guy feel like you're just thrilled to be held by him. It *moved* me. I feel like I've somehow been…cleansed."

There was something weird about a guy who could say such things so lightly.

"Are you trying to say you want to do it again?"

"That's not it. Don't take it that way."

"Gotcha."

"Hey."

"What?"

"Are you sleeping with Kunisada?"

This really took me by surprise. But there was no point in hiding anything from him. "That's a pretty bold thing to ask. Ten years ago we were. It was a case of transference and countertransference. But now we're just patient and therapist. I don't feel a thing for him."

"That's a lie. If you didn't feel anything for him there wouldn't be any need to see him." This felt like a stab. "The Professor says it's awful for him. He said you treated him terribly ten years ago. Said you seduced him, then suddenly lost interest, got grossed out, and finally tossed him aside like garbage. I wouldn't blame him if he held a grudge, but instead he's trying to help you." Then he added, enviously, "You're a karmic one."

Karmic just might be the best way to put it, I thought. This guy seemed to know me inside and out.

He continued, "That bastard just mentioned my name to you so he could show you off to me. I know him, he's a dirty old sado-masochistic wolf. He's real good at putting on the sheepskin, but really he's an animal unable to control his lust. He's probably imagining us sleeping together right now, torturing himself and whacking off at the same time."

I laughed again. "Come on, he's not that bad."

Yamagishi replied in a voice like ice. "You're not as smart as I thought."

"Why?"

"You've forgotten the most important thing."

"What?"

He put his arm on me as if to pin me down. "Well, when you dumped Kunisada ten years ago, you may have dealt him quite a blow. But all he got was a broken heart—at worst. You don't even realize how *you* were treated. *You're* the one who really got hurt."

"Me?" How's that?

"It's obvious, isn't it? You had a pact with Kunisada when you started analysis. It's the patient's right to experience transference. He had an obligation to protect you. Even if you were to strip your panties off right there and jump him, he should have controlled himself in order to protect you. That was his duty as a therapist. He abandoned that duty. He abandoned *you* so he could satisfy his own desires. You didn't do anything wrong. He hurt you. And you don't even know it. You're just not trying to see it. Listen, sex with your therapist is like incest. It's like sleeping with your father. You're the one who got hurt. Wake up."

Incest. It shook me.

I'd had the vague feeling that there was something I'd been avoiding, but I just hadn't been able to put my finger on it. Now it had been thrust in front of my face. *Calm down. What exactly is Yamagishi saying? This is very important. He's just told you something vital. You have to think about this. What did you do ten years ago? What exactly happened? You need to remember. You can't close your eyes to it.*

I recalled what Kunisada had said that afternoon.

"Do you remember what you said to me ten years ago? You said you hated emotions."

That's right. I'd been interested in psychology precisely because I'd felt I didn't have real emotions. I wanted to know what kinds of things people thought and felt. And I'd been told, "First you have to know yourself."

And so I'd started analysis. But my relationship with Kunisada had failed. And I'd lived ten more years without really knowing myself. What was it I'd really wanted to know—what had been bothering me?

I felt cool lips nibbling at my earlobe. Yamagishi's voice was like a hypnotist's. "Leave the old fuck alone. Don't have anything to do with him. You've got power. Believe in your-self. Victory is yours."

Why did this guy know me so well? I hadn't seen him in ten years, and even back then we hadn't been especially close, so why was he able to tell me things about myself that even I hadn't noticed? I felt as if he could see through me. And I felt, somehow, that I could understand him in turn, too.

"Who are you?" I couldn't keep myself from asking. He stopped what he was doing and thought for a while. I could almost hear his hard drive. He was like a machine, like a com-puter. That was why I felt at ease with him.

"Me? I'm... well, I'm the future of a decade ago."

"And what's that supposed to mean?"

He spoke as if to himself. "The future and the past are homologous. Mine are, so are yours. Ten years ago, we were in a similar place. Only, you were fenced in by that dirty old man and couldn't see the world around you. But I could see you."

I remembered what Ritsuko had said. *The two of you are alike, you're just on different vectors.*

Ten years ago, I'd been the one to tell Kunisada I wanted to be analyzed. At the time, his book was making a big splash in the media, and even though he was only an assistant professor then, he was a star on campus. Everybody knew of him. His lectures were joke-laced and interesting, and he exuded the confident air of a person who'd caught life's tailwind. He was genuinely attractive.

Every once in a while there'd be something in his attitude that suggested that he was interested in me. During lectures, he seemed to take special notice of me, calling on me often. I didn't know why he'd noticed me, but I was pleased that an older man, especially one as respected as he, had his eye on me. Without a moment's hesitation, I chose him as my academic advisor, and began to take an inordinate interest in clinical psychology.

My interests were always those of the man I liked. I'd always try to get into whatever he was into. And I'd always try to get good enough at it so he'd praise me. I was like a child, studying hard just to get her parents' approval.

I wanted Kunisada to pay attention to me. I wanted to get in deeper and deeper with him, so he wouldn't look at anyone else. And so I'd asked to undergo educational analysis with him. That way, we'd be forced to spend time alone. Sealed off in a private room, our relationship couldn't help but become intimate.

In those days, Kunisada was always surrounded by students who hung on his every word. He was a celebrity, appearing in lots of magazine interviews, and his students always wanted him to go out drinking with them. There were a few girls who seemed to have crushes on him, but I never heard any rumors of him getting involved with students. He was timid, afraid of any scandal that might get in the way of his career.

But I could tell right away that he had a weakness for women. Sometimes he went out drinking with a group of us, and he'd take the seat next to me and start asking me about my relationships with men. He was almost rude in the way he solicited my views on love. And sometimes when he was drunk he'd start to make provocative remarks.

"Yuki, I think you have a father complex."

We were all squeezed around a small table in a crowded bar. His thigh and mine were touching.

"Really? What makes you say that, Professor?" I pouted coyly. The other students at the table were all drunk and rowdy.

"You don't trust men, do you? And yet, when a man tries to get close to you, you're afraid of being disliked, so you force yourself to go out with him. Am I right?"

I denied it, but the fact was he'd hit the mark. I was never very good with guys. I didn't know how to maintain proper distance. When a guy would come on to me, I couldn't say no. I'd always end up sleeping with him. And I'd always regret it later.

The only time I could relax was when I was having sex. As soon as that physical contact disappeared, I'd feel uneasy again. I craved a strong, protective presence. That was why I was never satisfied with guys my age—their embrace was too shallow. They were selfish and I never felt that they loved me, except during sex. They always left me feeling starved. I'd never gone out with anybody I felt was right for me. They were all wrong. It got to be too much, and I decided that as long as I could have sex when I needed it, that would be enough. Guys I went out with would always ask, "What could you possibly be thinking?" But I myself didn't know.

Because I didn't know myself. I wanted to find out how this professor, this older man, saw me. I wanted him to define, in his words, what "Yuki Asakura" meant to him. Maybe then I'd be able to feel safe. And so I wanted him to notice me, to love me. I wanted to be defined and educated by an authority figure.

"My father was a sailor. He was never around when I was a kid."

Kunisada didn't seem too interested.

"Is that why I have a father complex, do you think? Do I have trouble getting along with men because I don't know my father very well?"

Sometimes, Kunisada seemed less a psychologist than a streetcorner fortune-teller. "Well, anyway, your family situation seems fairly complicated. That much I can tell."

This was when things were really bad between my eccentric brother and my ultramacho father. "How could you tell?"

I just can, he replied. He was drunk, and his ears were flushed. He never could handle liquor. When he talked he would get little glistening flecks of foam at the corners of his mouth. "I observe the students I'm interested in."

"Huh." I remember the sudden painful longing I felt then.

"Are you interested in me, Professor?"

"That I am."

"But why?"

He thought for a minute, and then said, "There's something special about you. A certain sensibility."

Kunisada's attachment to my body bordered on the obsessive. He licked every inch of it. He opened my folds and fingered me so much it felt like I was being turned inside-out. I had the feeling I was being made over. It wasn't a bad feeling. Sometimes I wondered if I was a pervert, to enjoy being used in such a way. I thought the man loved me. I was happy that a grown man was so obsessed with my body.

Kunisada was always complimenting me on my feel for counseling—not that I really had any feel for it. And he was always praising my body. Body and mind, I felt fulfilled by the man, and I think I was really happy.

Once the sex started, the analysis began to fail little by little. Whenever he saw me, Kunisada would get aroused. We even had sex in his office at school—any number of times. Although it might not be quite accurate to say we "had sex."

The more we petted each other, the more hesitant he seemed to enter me. He'd stroke my genitals, suck on my nipples, and masturbate.

"Why do you do that, Professor?" I'd ask.

"I feel sorry for you. I mustn't violate you," he'd answer.

What did he mean, he felt sorry for me? Self-centered man. It turned out he was a sado-masochist. For him not to enter me was his kind of sex. He got a kick out of it.

"I'm an awful man, to make such a lascivious woman out of you," he'd mutter stupidly, all the while saying how wet I was, how obscene I was, poking inside me with a finger and jerking his penis until he came. He liked to rub his sperm all over my breasts. In spite of that, I felt a curious fulfillment in being accepted by him—being kept and tamed by him.

After a while, however, he seemed to have decided he needed to control me emotionally, too.

One day, completely out of the blue, he began to tell me about somebody he'd once loved who'd died in a car accident. To this day, I don't know if she was real or just made up.

Kunisada had taken me for a drive on the Tokyo-Nagoya expressway. At the Atsugi interchange we headed toward Odawara, on the coast a few hours south of Tokyo. He said there was someplace he wanted to take me.

"There's something I haven't told you," he said affectedly. We'd just come from a love hotel, and I was really sleepy.

"What is it?"

"There's a certain place where a shard of my past is buried."

Whenever his fantasies started to rear their heads, his speech became really theatrical. He took me to a small intersection near the old castle in Odawara. It was late on a foggy winter night, and nobody was around. The mist diffused the red and green of the streetlights.

My lover died here, he said. I recalled that Kunisada was originally from Odawara. *If she'd lived, my life would be different now. I might have been the one who killed her. Whenever I'm here, I tremble uncontrollably. I think my thoughts remain here, sealed in this place.* He was weeping as he told me these things. He seemed to be trying to impress me with the fact that someone besides me had a claim on his heart.

It was at that instant that the hammer of the gods whacked me over the head, and my attachment to Kunisada vaporized. I realized that there was no way I really loved him. Maybe I'd just been projecting onto him my image of an ideal father all along. With my own father mostly away, and having failed to construct for myself an image of true fatherhood, I must have imagined I'd found my ideal in this man, shallow as he was.

But a true father wouldn't try to manipulate his daughter's emotions with stories of a former lover. Kunisada had gone and dismembered our relationship, all out of some stupid desire to dominate me.

Without a word, I got out of the car.

"Yuki!" He called after me in shock, as if struck by the proverbial bolt from above. I didn't hesitate at all, but walked away down the dark street.

"Wait, Yuki, what's wrong?" He hurriedly made a U-turn. I started running. I didn't want to be with him anymore. The spell had been broken. The prince had turned back into an ugly frog.

He honked the horn as he drove after me. "What are you angry about, Yuki?" He was visibly shaken. He finally seemed to realize how royally he'd screwed up.

I stopped and said, "Go away. You make me sick."

His mouth fell open wide. I almost puked at the thought that I'd slept with the disgusting man.

Really and truly, just like that, it was over. Or, at least, I'd thought it was. But was it really? I haven't been able to love a man. No matter who I sleep with, no matter how good the sex, when it's over and I'm alone, I get a little depressed.

Absolutely. The future and the past are homologous.

Unless I change *now*, right now, all I have to look forward to is a future exactly like the past.

18

It was ten in the morning when I got back to my apartment.

After checking out of the Shibuya love hotel we'd gone to the Bunkamura arts complex for coffee before saying good-bye. By then, I was having fever and chills. Maybe the air conditioning in the hotel room had been turned up too high. My face was hot to the touch, my body was shivering. I could feel cold sweat oozing out of my pores. Worried, Yamagishi had hailed a cab for me. Before letting me go, he stuck his head in the window of the cab and asked me over and over, "Are you sure you're all right?" Until the cabby too was giving me a look of concern.

When I sank back into the seat of the taxi, pain shot from my left shoulder blade down to my waist. It felt like the aches that come with a cold. My body felt heavy and tired. The stairs of my building seemed to stretch for miles. I felt dizzy, and my legs wobbled. This wasn't just lack of sleep. Something was happening to me.

I took the zubrovka from the fridge and took a swallow straight from the bottle. I couldn't stop shaking. I was drenched with sweat and freezing. I changed and crawled into bed. Every joint hurt. I was exhausted. My face and head were burning up. I pulled a thermometer out of the drawer of my bedside table and took my temperature. A hundred and three.

Through my haze I realized this couldn't be just a cold. It seemed viral though, influenza perhaps. My body was under attack by a virus. It was fighting back with a fever. If it was influenza, I might die if I just let it go. If the virus got into my brain I'd get encephalitis. If it got into my lungs I'd get bronchitis. Your body could stand a fever like this only for a few days... I figured I'd better get to a hospital and have them give me something.

I wondered if thinking about death for so long had lowered my immune levels. It wouldn't have shocked me to find that my body had used up all the energy it needed to live. My leukocytes must be down... I felt strangely calm as I thought all this. *You've got to get up and get to a hospital. You can't stay like this, you mustn't stay like this,* someone was hollering, but I couldn't get my body to move.

In my feverish state, on the border between dream and reality, I called the hospital any number of times, or tried to summon a taxi. I got up, changed, and called a cab. I visualized it until I couldn't tell it apart from reality. *It's all right now, I've called a taxi.* Thoroughly convinced I'd called one, but actually having done nothing at all, I fell into a deep sleep. It felt like being pulled into the depths of a dark swamp.

The doorbell rings. Someone has come.

I drag myself to my feet and walk toward the door. The narrow hallway is swaying like a rope bridge. "Who is it?" No response. I squint into the peephole, but there's nobody there. Nervously I open the door. There's a bag beside the doorway. It looks like it's made out of synthetic leather; it's shiny and shaped like a gym bag. Puzzled, I pick it up. It's heavy. Not just heavy, but awkward. It feels like it's filled with liquid.

I bring it inside. When I set it on the living room floor, something begins to seep out. A reddish-black liquid. Startled, I look at my hand. It's clean.

Looking back at the bag, I can see something on the surface, almost as if it had a design embossed on it. It's the outlines of whatever's inside. I look closer. It's a face. It seems there's a human head inside the bag. That's why it's leaking blood. Probably somebody hid it in this bag right after cutting it off and then placed it outside my door.

The face pressing against the side of the bag from inside becomes clearer and clearer. It's the face of a middle-aged man. It looks like my father, or like Kunisada. It looks like it could be crying or laughing.

I have an inexplicable urge to look inside. I have to know whose head it is, no matter what.

I gingerly place my hand on the clasp, and then quickly open it. It looks like a pair of lips gaping open. I can see something like hair, matted with blood. The whole room is filled with the smell of putrefying blood. I turn the bag over and shake out the contents. With a dull thud, a stinky mass tumbles out.

My dream disintegrated and I woke up.

I felt as if something had grabbed me and was pulling me back from another world. My cell phone was ringing: *Eine Kleine Nachtmusik*. I reached for it, and felt the ache in my left shoulder-blade. My body creaked as if it were out of oil. My head hurt, and my ears were ringing.

"Hello?" No answer. "Hello? It's Asakura," I said, coughing, and finally heard a reply.

"What's wrong? You sound awful."

Ritsuko.

I'd been sleeping for twelve hours when I was awakened by Ritsuko's call. As soon as she saw me she called the hospital and then took me to the emergency room. They said it was, indeed, influenza.

Where had I picked it up? At the hospital where I'd met Yamagishi, or at the love hotel? Either seemed like the kind of place that'd be crawling with viruses. No doubt, viruses instinctively recognize people who are fascinated by death.

They put me on an I.V. and kept me in the hospital overnight. I was so feverish that I couldn't remember much about being checked in. Occasionally a sound or some other stimulus would bring me back to consciousness, but I had no will to get up. I just slept, thinking nothing.

It was a sleep so deep and empty that it made me wonder if this was what death was like. *A pupa probably sleeps like this in its cocoon. A fetus probably sleeps like this in the womb.* What precious healing sleep gives, so precious that we spend a third of our lives sleeping. All so we can go on living in our turbulent world, taking in its stimuli and weathering its incongruencies.

When I opened my eyes, I saw the white ceiling of the hospital room, and the I.V. tube, and wondered for a moment why I was where I was. I was confused, but I also felt strangely refreshed. I must have perspired a lot; I felt like I do after coming out of a sauna and lying down for a little nap. I felt so good I almost felt guilty.

In midmorning, Ritsuko came and took care of the check-out procedures. She put me in a car, took me home, and forced me back into bed.

As soon as I closed my eyes, I fell asleep. I was sleep itself. *So that's what I am, a creature of sleep.*

Ritsuko stayed by my side while I slept, watching over me like I was a little girl. Every once in a while she'd wake me up, and I'd open my eyes like someone just summoned back from the netherworld; I'd eat a little yogurt or rice gruel, drink some water, roll over and go back to sleep. Ritsuko told me later that for forty-eight hours, I did nothing but eat, excrete, and sleep.

I hadn't even dreamed.

It was a sleep to make me forget I existed.

"I was worried you might never wake up," Ritsuko swore when I woke up on the third day.

I felt clean and fresh, as if I'd been born anew. "I think my brain was reinitializing itself while I was asleep. It feels like some unnecessary stuff has been gotten rid of, and now there's some free space on my hard drive."

This made Ritsuko laugh. "Everything you do, everything you say…you're not like other people."

Since I could get up for a little bit at a time, I forced myself to get back to work. I watched the news, read the papers, followed the market, wrote, and just generally tried to get back to my daily routine.

I told Kunisada I had a cold and couldn't make it to our session. And really, I was in no shape to be out and about.

Kimura had called while I'd been on medication and sleeping. Ritsuko had taken his call.

"He said he was going for surgery the next day, but that it wasn't anything serious, so you shouldn't worry," she told me when I woke up. The whole thing with Kimura seemed like a forgotten dream—I felt nothing at all when she gave me his message.

"Did he say which hospital he was going to be in?"

"No."

He didn't want to tell me. So there was no point in me worrying.

"Is Kimura your boyfriend, by any chance?"

I laughed and fudged an answer. Was he my boyfriend? Good question.

"What kind of operation is he getting? What's wrong with him?" Ritsuko asked.

Well, he smelled like death. He had to get the source of the stench removed. Just like having blood-stained tiles taken out.

"He has intestinal cancer," I said, simply. Ritsuko nodded.

I gave no further thought to Kimura. Maybe I didn't want to think about him. I didn't worry about him, I didn't even wonder how he was doing. I had no interest in him whatsoever, I felt nothing—it was as if he had already ceased to exist. Even after I got well enough to get out of bed, I had no desire to call him or to visit him at the hospital. I certainly didn't want to see him.

Sometimes he did come to mind—it wasn't like I'd forgotten about him entirely. I just had no emotions for him at all. I'd remember him, like some piece of scenery I'd seen long ago on a trip, and then he'd disappear, a fragment of memory. That was the only way I ever thought about poor Kimura.

No, it wasn't just Kimura. Nobody could stay in my heart. Other people couldn't stimulate me. I'd pulled my plug from humanity. I hated messy human emotions.

Ritsuko came over every day and took care of me until I got better. How long had it been since anybody had looked out for me like that? If Ritsuko hadn't come over that day, I might have died there in my apartment—ravaged by fever, wandering between dream and reality, not drinking or eating, not seeing anybody...just like my brother.

She made Okinawan food for me. It was fantastic. Lots of pork and vegetables, a wonderful stock—as I ate I could feel it all immediately turning into flesh and blood. Ritsuko was a hard worker, and she cleaned my whole apartment. She scrubbed under the sink, cleaned the mildewy refrigerator, wiped the oil splatters from the oven fan, wiped the grease and dirt from the range top, and just generally cleaned everything she could get her hands on. Pretty soon the place was sparkling. It had come back to life.

"Sorry for making you do all this," I said sheepishly, watching her zip around the place.

"Not at all, not at all. Cleaning is a form of training." I'd noticed that "training" was one of her favorite words. Taking care of my plants, cleaning my apartment, nursing me back to health—to her it was all training. "All of a housewife's duties are training," she maintained. Cleaning, washing, child-rearing, nursing, plant-care, they were all important tasks by which one could "send off spirits."

"And what does that mean, sending off spirits?" I was finding it more and more amusing to listen to Ritsuko.

"Hmm. These days you'd probably call it ministering. Nursing a dying person and helping his or her spirit make it safely to the other world. There are lots of housewives who say, 'Why do I have to do all this, from sun-up to sundown? I've had enough of this crap.' But from the standpoint of cultural anthropology, housework is a form of self-mastery. Through such training women learn to pity souls so they can minister to the dying." She added, "Shamanesses say that people who meet the gods always have to go through a kind of purification first."

"Purification?"

"Mm-hmm. Before they encounter the gods, they suffer

an injury, or an illness, something auspicious. It's like a warning: you're going to be meeting gods, so you'd better prepare yourself. Yuki, your getting sick like this might be a purification. Maybe the Okinawan gods are trying to tell you to brace yourself, prepare yourself, if you're going to go meet them."

Ritsuko sure said funny things. But I had really come to like her. It had been a long, long time since I had felt so intimate with another person.

"Ritsuko, before you went to Okinawa to meet the *yuta,* did you go through a purification?"

"Well, sort of," she said, as she changed the towel on my icepack. "I lost something important."

"Really? What?"

She smiled and stuck out her tongue. "That's a secret."

19

It had been almost two months since I'd learned of my brother's death. It was about time for autumn breezes to blow, but instead, the violent heat of summer continued. Day after day in the high eighties. Global warming. Something was very wrong. There were toxins in the air we breathed and they made everybody hysterical. It seemed like summer would go on forever. Some man suddenly went crazy and started shooting people on the street. A mother got depressed and killed her children. Men killed themselves. Huge earthquakes happened in succession, and there was a nuclear accident in Tokai village, Ibaragi. September was sick.

It's tiring to live in such a chaotic world, even more so if your sensitivities are heightened. No wonder my brother had finally decided to cross to the Other Side. I could easily understand that from my little spot in the sweltering metropolis.

I'd gotten back to work. Every morning I watched the news on satellite and kept an eye on the global market. I had to resume my studies to get my CFP. Following stock movements and analyzing market conditions were welcome distractions.

An earthquake in Taiwan came as a blow to a Japanese

computer manufacturer. Watching the market made me realize how interconnected the world is. From the standpoint of finance, it's all one. Like the butterfly flapping its wings in China, a revolt in a small country in Africa sent out ripples that reached across the world.

An American hedge fund was buying gold, so the price of gold was skyrocketing. It had been falling since the middle of the year, dropping steadily to new lows, but now it was shooting back up again. The news reported that the company responsible for the Tokai nuclear incident was a wholly-owned subsidiary of Sumitomo Metal Mining. The accident came right in the midst of the gold price spike at a time when Sumitomo Metal Mining's stock was on the rise. My eyes were glued to the market reports, expecting their stock to dive now. I figured this would cause Japanese stocks as a whole to take a hit, leading to a yen sell-off.

I found it fascinating to watch prices rise and fall in real time as influenced by events. Especially as I wasn't actually buying or selling gold myself.

Sure enough, Sumitomo Metal Mining's stock fell right after the accident hit the news. But, surprisingly, by the next day the price had stabilized—somebody was propping it up. Other Japanese stocks didn't seem disturbed, either. Some major power was at work in the virtual world to stabilize the economy. The market had been jittery for a while, but now it seemed to be starting to relax. I hadn't seen anything like it in my ten years on the job. Was the financial world changing? Did it mean people were changing, too?

Those who spent their time crawling into the cracks of the human heart and analyzing old traumas couldn't hope to sense any of this. Housewives who tired themselves out all day taking care of the elderly before dozing off themselves couldn't either. Nor could the girls in Shibuya with their fake tans.

Different worlds existed parellel to each other. Everybody had a part in sustaining them. Playing some sort of role. Or maybe not. Maybe everybody everywhere belonged to just one of those worlds and applied their talents to sustaining that world. Some people used money to uphold the financial world, some people sent off spirits to prop up the metaphysical world.

And me? What role was I playing, in what world?

During the time she was nursing me, I told Ritsuko about my brother, little by little. How he'd died, what the undertaker had said, and about the handsome young man from the cleaning company. Why I'd gone to Kunisada for counseling. Why Kimura was in the hospital. I told her about everything that had happened. And about outlets.

"You know, it's strange," Ritsuko said. "People who deal with the dead are usually kind, for some reason. Meanwhile, people who deal with the living are usually warped. Psychology deals with the living, right? And don't you think most psychologists are kind of twisted?"

I nodded.

"I mean, think about it like this. We're all terminals connected to a host computer. We each have our own hard drive, but we're all connected to a host. We access the host by outletting ourselves. 'Outlet' is really a verb." According to Ritsuko, to outlet was to access the whole.

"So what's the host computer? What is it really?" What kind of thing could integrate the whole universe?

"Probably something more simple than you think. Memory, maybe."

"Memory?"

She explained that the host was the storage place of all the memories of every human being, the sum total of the memories of everything that had happened since life first appeared on earth.

"Sounds like science fiction."

"Maybe. People into spiritualism call it the Akashic Record. Anyway, isn't it fun to think about stuff like that, even if it's far-fetched?

"Tell me what you think of this. You know organ transplants are quite common today. Well, in America there was a case where a heart transplant patient found that he had inherited the memories of his new heart's donor. In fact, there've been several cases like that. Now, what if there really were, somwhere in this world, a host that stored all of humanity's memories? Maybe these people somehow accessed it and subconsciously downloaded their donors' memories. Doesn't that seem possible?"

Part of me was incredulous, but part of me was just enjoying hearing her talk. "Okay, okay, so why do I hallucinate about my brother? Does that have something to do with hosts and memories?"

She glanced at her watch. "I have to get going, so I'll give you the short answer. You see your brother because that's your talent." *Talent*. Yamagishi had used the word, too. She continued, "Why don't you try abandoning the psychological term 'hallucination'? What you see has meaning only to you. Calling them hallucinations is merely trying to fit yourself into a psychologist's classification. You're not sick. Far from it. Your problem is that you're too normal."

That made me laugh. "You're absolutely right. I second it, motion carried."

Ritsuko grinned and then left. I waved goodbye from my bed. The door banged shut. The room fell silent.

When I was alone, though, was when it tended to come over me. There, I could feel it. That pressure in my solar plexus, that agitation in the air. That headache like the one I got when I held a cell phone to my head for too long. That twitching at the corner of my eyes. I put my fingers to my temples, closed my eyes, breathed deeply, and then opened my eyes again.

My brother was sitting on top of the cabinet where I kept my phone.

"Please, go away."

I closed my eyes and thought about work, then opened them again. He was gone.

I got well enough to go out, but that only created more worries. I remembered all sorts of things I had to take care of.

I sort of had my mind on Kimura's surgery as the date approached. There was my therapy with Kunisada, my trip to Okinawa to meet a *yuta*, and then there was Yamagishi. Everything was up in the air. I didn't know how to handle any of it.

Then, out of the blue, Yamagishi came calling.

He didn't even telephone first, he just showed up. When I heard his voice through the intercom from the lobby, my ears started burning. It was a strange sensation, almost as if a boy I had a crush on had suddenly dropped by. Quite a shock. I opened the door to find a bunch of flowers thrust under my nose.

"What's this?" It was a bright bouquet of small sunflowers.

"Visiting the patient," he said.

I took the flowers with a thank you, and then suddenly he was hugging me.

"Ritsuko told me all about it, what an awful time you had after we met. I'm so sorry, making you catch the flu like that."

"Don't be stupid! It's not your fault I got sick. Don't be such a little boy."

"Yeah, but you were white as a sheet and clammy when you left. I was so worried that I called Ritsuko to tell her."

So that's why Ritsuko had called me. She hadn't told me it was Yamagishi's suggestion.

I showed him inside. As he came in, he made a little detour around the phone cabinet, staring at the bottom of it. Weird guy, I thought.

"Why don't you want to walk by there?"

He threw me a suspicious glance and said, "No special reason." Then he added, "I'm glad to see you're looking so well."

"It's all thanks to Ritsuko. She nursed me back to health. I want a wife like her."

He laughed and gazed around the room. He picked up and examined photos, knickknacks, whatever was in the bookcases and on my desk.

"Looks like you have girlish tastes, eh, Yuki?"

"Have you got a problem with that? Anyway, I'm sure you came here for a reason. Why don't you just come right out and tell me?"

He nodded. "Listen, I heard from Ritsuko that you've been picking up smells of death, and seeing hallucinations of your brother."

That threw me for a loop, but I answered honestly. "Yeah. I guess I can't hide that kind of thing from an expert on schizophrenia."

"Is it true that you sniffed out a friend's illness?"

Now I was at a loss. I didn't quite understand that myself. "I think that was just a coincidence. Probably."

"So is there anything else?" I shook my head. "Okay."

"Do you think I'm crazy?"

"Are you nuts? Of course not."

Still, ever since my brother's death, I was getting progressively worse at figuring out what was real. Yamagishi was playing with my brother's clock while he searched his hard drive. I could almost hear the hum of his motor.

"Listen, Yuki. Do you know the difference between a psychiatrist and a therapist?"

I hadn't expected the question and it made me miss a beat.

"Maybe I'd better rephrase it. What's the difference between a clinician who's gone to med school and one who's come out of a liberal arts program?"

We were drinking iced coffee. The milk I'd put in mine was drifting in a marble pattern. I didn't know what he was getting at. I said, "Only a psychiatrist can prescribe drugs. The therapist can't treat people scientifically."

"That's part of it. But that's not the most important difference. I only found out myself after I got out of psychology and went to med school. Medical students, in order to become healers, go through a purification process."

"Purification?"

"Right. The first step is dissection: they have to disembowel a cadaver. That's pretty rough, let me tell you, but you can't become a doctor until you've done it. It's a rite of passage, I realized. You have to learn by touch what it means for a human being to have died. Everybody tries to go about it with a brave face, you know, making small talk and everything, but when the cadaver is, say, a young woman, you get this indescribable, unendurable feeling. I really started wondering what it means to be alive. 'This hundred-and-ten-pound glob of flesh in front of me once walked around on two legs,' you think. It's miraculous. What's the power that keeps us alive? 'Cause when you're dead, you're just a sack full of guts."

Ritsuko had said the same sort of thing. Why was everybody around me so interested in the life force?

"Psychologists deal with essentially healthy people who just aren't feeling too well. Right? The therapist's job is to help normal people whose minds are just a little under the weather. That's what I hated about it. That wasn't what I wanted to do. So I entered med school."

What was he trying to tell me? Still, I sort of understood. I'd had more or less the same thoughts.

"Once I'd gone through my rite of passage, I began to realize that the work I was involved in was in some measure shamanistic in nature. I discovered that what I'd really been after was engaging my patients sympathetically. Unlike visitors to the counseling room, people who are hospitalized are all basically *possessed*. They're babbling incomprehensibly, or they're in convulsions, or they're delusionary, or they've just collapsed mentally. But no matter how far out they are, there is always meaning in those delusions. The meaning's just in a form that only the sufferer can understand. And in order for you to understand the meaning of someone else's hallucinations and delusions, you have to descend into their darkness. It's dangerous. People's subconscious minds are wild places. 'Here there be demons,' and all that. You might sustain psychological damage yourself by going in. It's a journey into the unknown, and it's risky. You see, it's not really medicine—it's shamanism. That's what I realized."

No wonder he got along with Ritsuko.

"I've gone to meet several people who are known as shamans. A lot of them engage in what can only be called treatment. I was overwhelmed. They heal patients instantly and dramatically. They do in ten minutes what it would take me ten years to accomplish. I don't know what makes their patients get better, but the fact is they do recover. Doctors have nothing on these people. But they're fickle—they pick and choose who they're going to heal. Supposedly they can't do anything for patients who aren't on their frequency. We doctors don't have the luxury of screening our patients. If it takes time, it takes time, and all we can do is be optimistic and wait. Sometimes, when you're treating someone, you can't help wondering if you're just spinning your wheels. It can take a decade to cure schizophrenia, depression, multiple personality disorder. And there's no guarantee you can actually cure them. But you do it because you have no choice. Plus, I actually like schizophrenics. People whose personalities are fragmented and dissolving can be really sweet. Innocent. Their emotional makeup is different. It's like they're computers that run on a different operating system."

I listened quietly to Yamagishi's spiel. Where was he going with this? I never knew with him.

"You're wondering if I have a point, I can tell. Sorry. To be honest I'm not sure myself just what I'm trying to say. Just that, based on my intuition as a psychiatrist, I don't think you're mentally ill. What's happening to you is something else entirely. Your brother's death somehow plugged you into something. When that happened, a different operating system started up. Power's starting to flow, but your consciousness is trying to hold it back. Yuki, I think you've been living unplugged for a long time. No, that's not quite it. It's more that you've been getting by on a drastically restricted power flow. You've only been able to manage it because you've got this tremendous spiritual strength. But I think that living on power saver like that has tired you out more than if you'd lived ten normal lives. I think that's why you never liked other people. Dealing with people requires extra power. Your brother was probably the same as you, but you're much stronger than he was. You've been able to handle enough energy to live a normal life. But now that forbidden switch has been flipped. The voltage is rising. I don't know what's going to happen to you now, Yuki. It's beyond my area of expertise. I can't help you much, but if you fall into a trance, come see me. That's an order. See no other doctor."

What was he talking about? Was this a prediction? A warning? "Are you saying my confusion will only get worse?"

He gave a weak shrug of his shoulders. "I don't know. I think it might. I've had several patients like you before. These days a lot of people think everything can be explained by trauma, but that's only if the psyche in question is running the same OS as most people. With a Windows psyche, maybe trauma explains everything, but with a Mac psyche, it doesn't. And recently, more and more people are running on different systems—I'm sure of that. They're extremely sensitive. They've got new ways of processing things. But there's no manual yet for their OS. No applications that'll run on it. So people think they're malfunctioning, or full of bugs. Of course—they're still in development. Who knows, they might be beta versions."

I'd had enough. I interrupted him. "I have no idea what you're talking about."

Yamagishi still looked as if he had something to say, but I sealed his lips with mine. I'd been wanting to do this. It was quicker this way. I understand a man when I'm connected to him that way.

With our tongues entwined I took off my clothes and unbuttoned his shirt. As he held me, I realized I'd been wanting to see him for a long time. This man was anxious about me, that much was clear. And that was enough. I straddled him and made quick, athletic love to him. After only a few gyrations of my hips he hurriedly pulled his penis out of me and came. As he was wiping his semen off the floor with tissues, I could see that he had tears in his eyes.

"Why are you crying?" I asked, stroking his hair.

He curled up like a child and said, "When we make love, it brings back all these lost memories."

I held him and kissed him gently.

That evening Ritsuko called, so I told her that Yamagishi had come over earlier. Her apology for telling him my secret was offhanded. "My loose lips would sink a ship."

"But why didn't you tell me that Yamagishi had asked you to call me when I was sick?"

Ritsuko sighed. "It wasn't like I was keeping it from you. I just didn't see the need to tell you. Or are you saying it would have made you happy to know Yamagishi was worried about you?"

"Come on, that's not it." I didn't care for her tone.

"Yuki, you may think I'm way out of line here, but I'm going to butt in anyway. Yamagishi's married. He has a wife. Keep that in mind, okay?"

I had a curious feeling in my stomach, as if I'd swallowed something I shouldn't have. I hadn't known he was married. It had never even occurred to me to ask. But of course, he was at an age where I might have expected him to be married—certainly there was nothing surprising about it.

"So what?" I said.

"I'm just saying."

"Hmm. Well, bye."

After I hung up I realized I didn't know why Ritsuko had called in the first place. I thought she'd call right back, but she didn't phone again that evening.

The day of my appointment with Kunisada has come. I've been nervous all morning. I've done a lot of thinking about what I'll say when I see him again, but I haven't settled on anything.

I show up at the counseling room as usual, but when I go in I find a notice. *We'll be meeting in my office today*.

So I walk down the dim hallway to his office. Being in that room always reminds me of sex with Kunisada. Does he know that—is that why he switched rooms?

I knock and enter to find Kunisada in a swivel chair as usual, rocking from side to side. "Come in, come in," he says, and motions me in with his eyes. I expect him to order me to take off my clothes right there in front of him. But he just tells me to sit. Then, in a strong, professional tone, he says, "I imagine you're ready to resolve things."

What kind of resolution does he have in mind? Between him and me? Or between me and my brother?

"I have to break your seals for you," he says, with a faint smile. I'm afraid. What does he intend to do to me? I try to stand up to run away, but my legs won't move. Before I know it, Kunisada's behind me, clutching my breasts with his talon-like fingers and pushing me back into the chair.

"Now for some *real* counseling," he says, letting his tongue wander down my neck. His tongue is strangely cool, like a snake's. When it touches my nipples, I feel a pleasure like numbness spreading through the lower half of my body.

"Open up." I spread my legs. "Wider." I spread them wider, feeling utterly defenseless. "That's it. That's the way to open yourself up. Return to your true self. Your true, vicious, obscene self."

Something long, thin, and sleek pushes its way into my vagina. A chill shoots through into the core of my body. He is using his fountain pen. He's rubbing my genitals with the cap, like he's churning cheese.

"Go ahead, say it," he whispers in my ear. "Say you want to kill your family." There's a muffled sound, and spider-web cracks appear and dash across my chest. "You hate your family. You want to kill them. You hate your asshole father, your stupid mother, and your weak, spineless brother. You wish they were all dead. Admit it."

Maybe he's right.

"Voice those feelings. Break the seal. Only by doing that can you win back your true self." The snake's tongue is licking my closed eyelids. My lips. My ears. "Now say it aloud. 'Everybody, die! I don't need a family. Die, all of you!'"

I try to say it, but it's as if my language center is locked. I can't find words.

"What's wrong? Say it. It's what you wanted all along— you wanted that burdensome brother of yours to die, didn't you? Spit out your true feelings. It'll all be over then. You'll be a new Yuki. It's easy. Just say the words." The fountain pen, hard in my vagina, is getting bigger and bigger. Now it's Kunisada's penis. He's moving it regularly in and out of me, and Kunisada himself as he covers me is growing and shrinking like a shadow thrown by a flickering flame. And he keeps saying, like a hypnotist, "You wanted your brother to die. Admit it. Scream it out loud."

That's right, I think. I want to scream, and come. But when I try to shout *Die!* my throat is blocked by what feels like several clumps of lead.

"If you can't say it, I'll lend you my tongue." Kunisada's tongue comes slithering into my mouth. It smells raw, like some snake. The smell mingles with my brother's death-stench.

An instant later, I see my brother. He's standing at the unmanned crossing, looking forlorn. The rails are trembling and groaning. A train's coming. He's going to be hit. He doesn't move. His lips are moving—he seems to be saying something. But I can't hear him over the noise of the train.

Run! There's a ghost at this crossing. You'll be taken away to the other side. You'll die! I raise my hands and scream: "Taka! Don't die!"

My own scream woke me up. I'd been crying in my sleep.

I sat up in bed, panting, fists clenched. My brother was going to die, he was dying—that fear wouldn't leave me. I was soaked with sweat and tears.

After a little while, I calmed down enough to realize that he was already dead. *You idiot. He's dead already. You went to his cremation. He's no longer of this world. He's nowhere.*

Suddenly, I felt a deep sense of loss. Loss is a void. It's momentary insanity. The loss of a person is the extinction of a world. A universe perished inside me.

I cried until dawn, the first time I'd cried since my brother's death.

I guess I really liked my brother. I wasn't just annoyed by him. Why hadn't I mourned his death until today?

I wanted to reach Kimura.

I tried his home, his office, and his cell phone, but got no answer. I left a polite message on each. If he was alive, I was sure he'd hear one of them. And if he was dead, well, I guess I'd never see him again. Imagining him dead didn't elicit any strong feelings. Would I cry later? Might I see the end of a world in Kimura's death like I did in my brother's? Who knew?

I just didn't understand my own feelings.

Kimura called back in the afternoon. It was more of a relief than it should have been to hear him sounding upbeat. I was strangely glad that he was still alive.

"So, you made it?"

"Thanks to you, I'm fit as a damn fiddle." There was something forced in his voice, though. He might have been putting on a brave face for me. He said he was still in the hospital, but that he'd be out at the end of the month. "The doctors were shocked. Usually, colon cancer doesn't present any noticeable symptoms until it's pretty far along, they said. Usually they have to take out the anus and the lymph nodes. In my case, they caught it early. They kept asking me why I'd decided to take the tests. I didn't know what to tell them. I couldn't very well say someone had told me I stank, right? They said it was a real miracle. Thanks to you, I'll be back at work next month."

So had that smell been coming from his bowels?

"Well, that's great." Even I could tell that my response was pretty tepid.

"What about you, Yuki? Sounds like you were closer to death than me." Kimura always put other people first.

"I'm better now. In fact, I feel better than I did before I got sick. I feel like my body did its spring cleaning."

"Well, I'm sure you were exhausted from everything you'd been through. It was probably good for you to just take it easy. Oh, hey, I'm on a payphone, and my card's running out. We may get cut off any minute."

I could hear faint sounds in the background on the other

end of the line—announcements and things. I said, "Listen, you didn't tell me anything about your operation until the last minute—was that because you thought I wanted it that way?"

"What do you mean?"

"You didn't even tell me which hospital."

"I didn't do it on purpose."

"Whatever. I'm not accusing you of anything. To be honest, I didn't worry about you one bit. I was so overwhelmed with my own problems I just couldn't spare a thought for yours. I felt it would just be exhausting to get involved in your life. *That's why you didn't contact me.* You're a ridiculously good guy, so you always know what I want, and you try to accommodate me."

I could hear him sigh. "Yuki, you think too much. I really didn't have any of that in mind."

"Well, whatever. But I'll warn you—no matter how much you lend me, I won't pay interest."

"What the hell are you talking about, Yuki?"

"I think I know why I smelled death on you. It was just a coincidence that it led to you being diagnosed. How could a tiny polyp in your intestines smell like death? It wasn't that. It wass because you remind me of my brother. You're too nice, you try to please other people, you try to do what they want—just like him. That's why I smelled the same thing from you. Now that I know, I'm all right. You don't have to have anything to do with me anymore."

"What do you mean, you're okay? I can't believe how self-centered you are."

The line went dead. His card must have run out.

I knew I shouldn't tempt Kimura anymore. If I'd saved his life without meaning to, that was enough. If we went on seeing each other, sooner or later he'd become a burden, and I'd wish him dead.

20

"Did you sleep with Yamagishi?"

Ritsuko's question came so suddenly that I almost coughed up my tea. She seemed worried that I might like him.

"Yeah," I said.

"I *knew* it," she said, recoiling. "You know, he said it would happen, way back when."

"What?"

"He said, 'Someday I'm going to have Yuki Asakura.' And he's obsessive—he sticks to things. Once he's made up his mind, he'll do anything, even if it takes ten years. You've got to admire him, almost."

Had Yamagishi really said something like that? "I don't even remember him from ten years ago. He's such an interesting guy, you'd think I'd remember him, but I just don't."

"That's because you only had eyes for that oversexed professor of ours. You didn't notice any younger men."

She was right. "So why did Yamagishi have his eye on me?" I'd been wondering about that.

"It wasn't only Yamagishi. They all had crushes on you. You were emitting pheromones. You were different from all us other girls—maybe you were more mature sexually. You didn't flirt with guys or anything, but you sure turned them on. Like some kind of prostitute."

Maybe I had. I could imagine.

"Yuki, you don't have female friends, do you?"

"Hmm, I guess you're right. You're about the only woman I know I'd call a friend, Ritsuko." It was an honest answer.

Ritsuko looked exasperated. She said, "You must be lonely," and lapsed into silence. Then, bracing herself, she set forth, "You know, Yuki, I thought you were special, I thought you had some kind of special spiritual grounding. That's why I was so excited about you. But I can see now that I was wrong. You're just depraved. You're an erotomaniac."

I was shocked. "Watch what you say."

She didn't back down. "Come on, I saw you. That night in the park in Shinjuku. I could hear you from the street."

I felt as if I'd had a bucket of ice water splashed on me. *So that really happened.*

So what did Ritsuko want with me? Why was she meddling? I could understand men once I connected with them. Women, I just couldn't understand.

"All right, let me ask you something."

"What?" Ritsuko looked apprehensive. For all her occasional boldness, she was a coward.

"Just why are you researching shamanism anyway? You used to be such a rationalist. What changed you?" I'd been wanting to ask that for a while. *I know I'm strange, but you're not exactly normal yourself, Ritsuko.*

"That'd take a long time to explain, and I'm not sure I feel like telling you yet. I don't think I'd be able to explain my experiences to you, not in your present condition. Part of you still looks down on me for being into fringe occult stuff. What happened to me, no matter how strange, in the end has meaning for me—and only me. You haven't experienced it, so it won't mean anything to you. I am the way I am today as a result of it, though. I don't have the energy to explain my experiences to someone who dismisses me as a weirdo. Testimonials like that testify to the power of the listener. Isn't that right, former psychologist wannabe?"

Seeing Ritsuko get angry at me, I finally understood. She'd been through something similar. Why hadn't I guessed? Some strange experience she couldn't understand had led her to seek answers from shamanism. And because she hadn't found any answers, she was starting to wonder if she was on the right track. She wanted to share her experiences with me, to compare notes with me, but I wasn't accepting my own experiences on a mystical level and that was upsetting her. Ritsuko was confused. She was trying to embrace the incomprehensible. Maybe we had that in common: we were both trying to accept the unacceptable.

"You're right, Ritsuko. Im sorry. Maybe I'm being obstinate, maybe I'm in denial. I don't know why, but I'm afraid that if I start accepting ideas like souls and gods now, I'll be evading the real reason for my brother's death. I don't want to do that. I want to know why I smell death, why I see my brother, and I don't want spiritualist answers. If I seem stubborn, that's because I'm forcing myself to face reality with my own ego. That's why I'm in therapy." I didn't think clinical psychology was the answer, but it was a weapon when the ego was threatened. Knowledge provides a way of overcoming oneself. Knowledge is another tool. That much I knew.

"Objection, Your Honor. Therapy is all about having a reliable counselor with whom to confront your emotional wounds in the context of a mutual relationship. Is that really happening with you and Kunisada? Objection Number Two: I think it's pretty tough to try to embrace death with just your ego. Science hasn't even explained what death is. How can you cram something as irrational as death into your ego and expect to be able to process it rationally? That's why humanity has always invented myths, dreams, afterworlds, gods. Look, I've spoken to a lot of shamans and shamanesses, and I've come to think that it would be a good thing if all the psychologists in the country just disappeared. People can heal their own psyches. They have the power. The more psychologists we have, the more people are going to believe that they can't heal themselves without someone else's help. Depending on the meddling-services industry is a sure road to ruin."

So she wanted all the counselors in the world to be gone? And this was from someone who had once wanted to enter the field herself. I wondered if it really would be a good thing, if we really could do without therapists. I could see what she was getting at, the meaning that lurked behind her words. I could understand it, but I couldn't verbalize it yet. So I didn't say anything.

"I could tell you just a little bit." I gave her a quizzical look. She grinned. "I mean, why I became interested in shamanism. As you know, I originally wanted to become a psychologist myself. I wanted to help people who were suffering. I wanted to understand the dark recesses of the human mind. It was what I'd wanted ever since I was a teenager. By the time I got to college I was sure it was my calling. It disturbs me to think about the way I was then. I was looking for sick people. I had this compelling desire to treat them. I was so arrogant."

There was nothing unique in that. People who want to handle other people's minds must first struggle with their own desire to dominate them.

"Then, in my senior year, I had a shocking experience. A girlfriend of mine suddenly lost her mind. We'd been together only the day before—we'd gone to see a play in Kinokuniya Hall in Shinjuku. It was *Hymn*, by Soh Kitamura, kind of a fantastic, mystical play. It's set on Earth after a nuclear holocaust, and it's a really sad, beautiful piece. We came out of it deeply moved, and just wandered around the streets of Shinjuku for a while. She was on a high—excited from the play, I figured. She was that type, you know, easily moved. We had a drink in a bar in Kabuki-cho and then parted. I didn't notice anything out of the ordinary with her.

"I got a call early the next morning. 'I've got it,' she said. 'I understand, I understand everything.' It's the kind of thing you hear a lot from people in the early stages of schizophrenia, right? I was immediately suspicious—I just had an intuition that something wasn't right. She was all keyed up, talking nonstop. 'Hey, Ritsuko,' she said, 'Trees are the world's antennas! I realized that after watching the play last night. Trees receive vibrations from outer space. The biggest antenna in the world is in Findhorn. It's the rhinoceros's horn.' She kept spewing incomprehensible stuff over the phone. I hung up and rushed over to her room. When I got there she was busy throwing all her belongings out the window. She'd totally snapped. I called the police and had her taken into protective custody, because she was going wild. I mean, she'd picked up this huge wardrobe and was trying to get it out the window. I don't know where she'd gotten the strength—it was a measure of how beside herself she was. She'd probably been up all night, in agony. I figured I couldn't wait for something awful to happen, and I also knew I couldn't restrain her alone. They put her in a straitjacket and marched her to the hospital, shot her full of tranquilizers, and kept her there for a year. When she got out, she was in a daze from all the medication. She said she'd been given electroshock therapy, too, and her memory was in shreds. She wanted to transfer to a better hospital, but when you've been committed involuntarily, you don't even have the freedom to request a transfer.

"I spent all my time wondering what had happened to her mind. There I was, so proud of myself for knowing psychology, and I hadn't been able to save her. I felt tremendous guilt. I started trying to solve the riddle of her psyche, starting with an investigation of her upbringing, her family. And of course, the more I rummaged through the drawers of her life, the more possible causes I found for her insanity. Mobilize enough traumas and you have yourself a mental patient. But something didn't seem right to me. My efforts to find reasons, to label and justify her illness, weren't meant to help her—it wasn't for her sake that I was dissecting her.

"Then one day, in a description of Siberian tribal myths, I came across the idea that plants are antennas. The same thing my friend had said in her delirium. Even if it was just a coincidence, it seemed an awfully strange one to me. I began to consider the things she'd said to me. Just like you've been doing with the riddle of the outlet. And it just got more and more intriguing. She'd told me that 'the world's biggest antenna is in Findhorn. It's the rhinoceros's horn.' Well, it turns out there really is a place called Findhorn. It's in Scotland. The name was originally "Found Horn." Evidently it used to be home to a lot of deer, and people came there to look for antlers.

"But she'd mentioned a rhino's horn, not a deer's. It didn't make sense. Findhorn is world-famous as sacred ground, as a place where miracles happen. The ground is barren, but for some reason they grow huge vegetables there. People who go there find themselves mysteriously healed. But no matter how much I read up on the place, I found no mention of an antenna. So I finally went there myself. And boy, was I in for a surprise. There's a commune there, filled with people from all over the world seeking healing. In the center of town there's this place called the Universal Hall, and when I went in I found a quilted tapestry on the wall. And on it was embroidered a unicorn. Depending on how you looked at it, it sort of looked like a rhino. I asked a staff member what it was supposed to symbolize. And she said it was a revelation that the center's founder had received in a dream. But it wasn't the kind of thing that could be made public—it wasn't the kind of symbol meant to convey anything to the outside world. There are very few people who know about the unicorn. Now, isn't that a coincidence? Needless to say, my friend had never been to Findhorn. So why had she said that the world's biggest antenna was the rhino's horn—the unicorn's horn? Was it just a coincidence? It couldn't be. And then, Findhorn is surrounded by a forest of tall cedars, and I was told that their pointed tips were antennas to gather God's love. Everybody there believes that the forest is filled with spirits. I even met people who said they'd seen some."

Having come that far in her story, Ritsuko paused and sipped at her tea, now cold. I waited for her to go on. My fingertips had already started to tingle and tremble, as if they were conducting electricity.

"I started to wonder just what madness was. Was my friend really crazy? Was she really delusional? What are delusions, really? Then I came across the Okinawan *yuta*. It turns out that most of them had been in pretty bad shape psychologically before becoming *yuta*. The kind of shape that would have any of us calling the cops to have them taken away. But in the community there on Miyako Island, they call women like that *kamidari*, and accept them as special people who are going to do the work of the gods. After their derangement passes, these women return to life as shamanesses and work at healing people's minds. I started wondering if I had inadvertently taken away my friend's power…you know, by having her forcibly committed. I started to think that maybe we still have a lot of people like that around us today, only they're locked up as lunatics and kept on medication. And so ever since then I've been doing research on shamanism."

"Are there a lot of people like that?"

"Which—mental patients or shamanesses?"

I sighed. The vagueness of the distinction between madness and reality was something that nobody who hadn't experienced it could truly hope to understand. I didn't even know if my dead brother had been sane or insane. Boundaries are hazy when it comes to the mind.

Ritsuko continued. "Before the mind awakens to a higher order of consciousness, it sometimes goes through a period of confusion. Some scholars distinguish that state from mental illness and call it a 'spiritual emergency.' Okinawan women who are in the process of becoming *yuta* always go through it. On the way to gaining their shamanistic powers, they pass through a state that we would call derangement. Here they would be diagnosed with mental illness and hospitalized. Like my friend. Now, during spiritual emergencies, visual or olfactory hallucinations sometimes occur. They're often triggered by a near-death experience or the death of a relative—times of psychological crisis."

I finally got what Ritsuko was trying to say. "So is that what you thought was happening to me?"

"Well, duh. You're analytical all right, but I can't tell if you're sharp as a tack or dumb as a box of hair. I can't tell whether you work by instinct or by reason. That's what attracted me to you, as a research subject. I thought maybe you were someone who would emerge from your spiritual emergency as a new type of shamaness. Shamanism has to evolve, too, you know. A traditional shamaness wouldn't be able to cut it in the big city—she wouldn't be able to link her netherworlds with this one."

I held up my hands for her to stop and said, "Sorry, but I've never had the slightest paranormal talent—no premonitions, nothing."

"I wonder about that. You don't seem to know yourself very well. Don't you have the ability to read other people's feelings like you're reading a book? Isn't that ESP? You're afraid of being deluged by others and the pain and madness that would result, so you keep your eyes shut. I'm sure your brother was the same way. All that's different between you two is the way you've expressed it, and the way you've protected yourselves. Everybody's different: two people can live in contrary ways and still have the same goal in mind. You've succeeded in lowering your blinds, but your brother, who failed, wasn't able to awaken to anything beyond himself."

Now she was sounding like Yamagishi. He'd said my brother and I were the same, too. He'd said I wasn't plugged in all the way.

"The outlet is *you*."

"Me?"

"Yes, you. You're searching for a way to harmonize with this world."

A warning whistle broke the silence.

I'm at the unmanned railroad crossing again.

Why does this place keep coming up?

I'm standing at the dark crossing with my brother and my mother. It looks to be around dawn.

My brother and I are still little. I'm about three, so Taka must be in eighth grade or so. Mom is clutching us close to her, one on each side. Her arm's around my neck so tight it hurts. I'm crying and screaming, really upset. I can feel the vibrations of a distant train coming to me through the air. Mom means to throw herself in front of that train. I bite her arm. She suddenly thrusts me away. She clenches my brother's hand and pulls him toward the tracks. He meekly allows himself to be dragged. A horrific reddish-black mist is shooting out of the top of Mom's head. I yell, "No, don't!" My brother looks back at me and shakes his head sadly. I grab hold of Mom's leg and sink my teeth into her calf. I have to save Taka. If I don't, she's going to take him away. Mom's eyes are rolled back in her head, and every time she moves another spurt of crimson steam shoots up from her head.

She desperately tries to break free of me, shaking her leg and stamping her foot. I realize she's no longer in her right mind. My brother is trembling like a leaf. He's pale as a corpse. The shaking spreads through his body and gets so violent that he can hardly stay standing. He hugs himself to try to get it under control, but he can't stop trembling. Now his eyes are rolled back so that all I can see are their whites, and he's drooling.

Trembling, he begins to walk toward the crossing, and the train is bearing down on him.

"Yuki, are you all right?"

I'd slipped into a daydream. I was weeping.

"Sorry. I had a flashback."

Ritsuko handed me a handkerchief.

"I don't know what came over me. I had completely, totally forgotten about it. It only came back to me just now."

I seemed to be responding somehow to what Ritsuko had been saying. I wasn't in control of myself.

"What did you remember?"

What, indeed? It felt like something that had really happened. "When I was little, my mother tried to kill herself by throwing herself in front of a train at a railroad crossing. She tried to take us with her. My father's violence was really out of control back then, and she was always saying she wanted to die. She was emotionally exhausted, neurotic. And my brother responded by having an attack of his own—he threw himself in front of that train, of his own will."

"What happened to him?"

"He survived. The train stopped. The engineer probably saw the three of us struggling. But it was a close call—I mean, that train stopped without an inch to spare."

My brother had once said to me, *You're strong. I envy you.* At the time I hadn't understood his meaning. I'd never considered myself a particularly strong person. Maybe he'd been thinking of how I fought Mom then.

"Your brother was a very delicate person, wasn't he?"

"Phew, Ritsuko...I think you're right. My memories of him being violent had made me forget. Yes, my brother was a really kind person. He was gentle. Too much so. That's why he'd tried to shoulder Mom's sufferings all by himself."

How could I have forgotten? My brother was susceptible to the emotions of those around him. That always confused him. He never knew where he left off and where someone else began.

He wasn't sick at all. He was just born like that. That's why he'd asked me, over and over, *Hey, Yuki, when that boy is unplugged, what is he seeing? Do you think he feels anything? Is he asleep, is he awake, can he hear anything? What's the un-plugged world like? What do you think, Yuki?*

21

When I stepped up to the nurses' station and mentioned Kimura's name, a young woman at the desk who was writing a memo gave me a strange look. Our eyes met and she bowed almost imperceptibly before she went back to work. But her look had had a peculiar emotional charge. Maybe she had a crush on Kimura.

He was in a large shared room with six beds. When I entered he was sitting on the edge of his bed by the window reading a magazine. Soft autumn sunlight streamed in through the window. He'd been shaving, and he looked neat. His long fingers were as graceful as ever. He seemed healthy.

"Hey," I said. He looked up, and then sprang off the bed. I stifled a laugh: some people literally jumped when they were startled.

"What's with the sudden visit?"

"No special reason, just thought I'd see how you're doing."

The other patients were grinning at Kimura's discomfiture. They were watching TV with earphones, or sleeping, or reading. The air was filled with particles of a wide variety of scents. But the stench of death was not among them, which came as a relief to me. I invited Kimura to come outside with me.

We sat on a sunlit bench in the courtyard. It was a little chilly out, and there was nobody around.

"So, I get out tomorrow."

"I know. You told me. You look healthy, too."

He was dressed in hospital-issue green. The trousers were too short, and his ankles stuck out comically.

"I came here today because there's something I want to test."

Immediately, he replied, "The smell, I bet."

"Huh?"

"You want to test your nose, right? I figured you'd come."

"Actually, you're right. Sorry."

"No need to apologize. I understand how you must be feeling. I'm curious, too."

"I had no intention of seeing you again, you know. But I just had to make sure."

He looked downcast. "Why don't you want to see me?"

"Hmm…I can't find the words for it. I just don't like you that way. I'm not interested in you. I'm afraid of using you just because you're so nice to me."

Why weren't there better words? Language isn't a very developed means of expression.

"Shit. I guess you're right. No matter how hard I try, I'm not much use to you," Kimura lamented. I said nothing—I'd made up my mind to listen to him today, to hear what he had to say. "You're much stronger than I am, Yuki. I guess I always knew that I was the only one being helped. I'm too weak to be able to help you. Just knowing you, I could tell you were hurting in places I couldn't see. Even sitting right next to you like this, you're in a different world. Why is that? I've never had to feel like that. You're like a ghost, Yuki. Sometimes I don't think you're of this world. But I think that's what I always liked about you."

"Well, thanks." I'd felt the same thing. Even when Kimura and I shared the same space, we were wandering around in separate worlds.

"One more thing. You seem to think otherwise, but I don't know of one man who speaks badly of you. All the guys that I know who've been with you really like you."

"Cut it out. You're embarrassing me."

"I know why, too. When they're, you know, together with you, they feel fulfilled, like they're reliving some childhood moment of happiness they'd forgotten. They come out of it with new courage. I can't describe it very well, but there it is."

He was talking about sex, and he was having trouble putting it plainly. Was it an honor to have my lovemaking praised that way? I wasn't sure what to think.

Meekly, he brought his face close to mine. "So, anyway. Do I still smell?"

I sniffed. I could detect various medicinal odors, and a certain sourness mixed in with his bodily fluids, but no stink of death. "I can't tell. Can I get you to exhale?"

He breathed out. More of that sour pharmaceutical smell, but nothing else.

"It's gone. That's good, isn't it?"

But there was only sadness in Kimura's eyes as he gazed at me.

I said, "I'll be going now."

We didn't exchange a word as we walked to the lobby. There was a cherry tree by the entrance, and its leaves were starting to turn colors. Autumn was progressing. I shook Kimura's hand and said, "See ya."

I'd almost forgotten! "Oh, yeah, you know that cute nurse, the one with the teardrop mole?"

Kimura fumbled with words.

"I think she likes you," I told him.

I waved and headed home. Behind me Kimura muttered, "Damn you, Yuki."

I went to the bus stop in front of the hospital. An elderly couple was there, waiting for the bus. I got in line behind them, and as I stood there, I was suddenly overcome by sadness. I didn't love Kimura—so why was I sad? I was sure the feeling would pass. By the time I got off the bus I would've forgotten all about him, I told myself. Emotions were always ephemeral. All I had to do was wait for them to pass.

The bus came, and I filed on after the old couple. A recording told us to take a ticket. The old lady took one, but the man with her didn't.

"Uh, you forgot to take a ticket," I said to him, and the old lady turned around, thinking I was talking to her. At that moment, the old man disappeared.

"Oh, ah, the, uh, behind you…" I stammered, then clamped my mouth shut. The driver and the other passengers were looking at me strangely. "I'm sorry, never mind."

My heart was pounding. I took my ticket and looked for a seat. The old woman had already sat down, and I took a seat across the aisle from her. I glanced over at her, out of the corner of my eye, and there he was. She'd sat down in the aisle seat, and the window seat was occupied by the old man. He had white hair and a white beard, and he wore a gray woolen suit and a brown vest. I could see him quite clearly. He didn't look the least bit like a hallucination or a ghost. He looked alive.

I knew people would get suspicious if I stared, but I couldn't help myself. He sat very close to the woman, looking straight ahead.

My palms felt clammy. The old woman gave a melancholy sigh. And on her breath I could smell death.

What's going on? Who is this old man I see? Calm down and think things through. Take a deep breath, look again, and then figure it out. Five stops later, the old woman pressed the Stop Requested button. When the bus came to a halt she stood and made her way toward the door. Her movements were slow. She looked very ill. The old man stood up and followed her. He walked normally, but without a sound. No rustle of clothes, no footsteps.

The old woman got off the bus, and just as the old man was about to follow her out, the door slammed shut. I covered my eyes. He could have been crushed. When I opened my eyes again, the bus was already moving. On the sidewalk, the old woman was tottering along, with the man right beside her.

"Sorry, I need to get off! Please stop the bus!"

The driver opened the door and I got off the bus.

It was too real, it couldn't be a hallucination. And yet, I knew that the old man probably didn't exist. Only I could see him. Was I daydreaming? But his image was so clear—I wasn't even afraid. It just felt strange.

Or maybe everybody on the bus had seen him. Maybe everybody had seen him and just pretended they hadn't. No, that couldn't be. The driver had almost crushed him with the door. If he'd done that knowingly, he'd be a murderer.

The old man had disappeared at the door and he'd reappeared once the bus started moving. One thing was clear: he was not material. So what was he? The word "spirit" came to mind, but I chased it away. There was no such thing as spirits.

I followed the elderly couple.

They were just about to disappear down a residential side-street. They were walking slowly, so it wasn't hard for me to catch up with them. They snailed along in single file, and in their wake they left a sticky, reddish-black slug trail. It came to me that the old woman was about to die. I knew it intuitively.

The man had to be her dead husband. As the woman's time drew near, she was beginning to resonate with her dead husband's energy.

They went into a little house at the end of the street. The

old woman opened the door, and the old man disappeared into the house right along with her.

Clouds raced across the sky at dizzying speed. The sun shone dazzlingly on the roof of the house. The house was so strongly backlit that all I could see was its silhouette.

I stood there dumbstruck and forgot the way back.

Where am I? It seems like the residential neighborhood I was in just a minute ago, and then again it doesn't. Buildings that all look alike line the streets. Each house is flat, and light glares off every one of them. There's a road. But I can't see where it goes. All meaning has been chipped away from the scenery. This is a road, this is a telephone pole, this is a gate, this is a mailbox...but I don't know what any of them does. They're just things. I don't know their meaning.

It's almost as if I'm on a movie set. Everything's fake, everything's flat, everything's meaningless. I wonder if I'm dreaming. Maybe I'm caught in a two-dimensional comic-book world, like in a dream I once had. If it's a dream, I'll wake up from it eventually. But what if I don't—will I just be left here, in this world, forever?

No, it's no dream. I'm just confused. That's it, I'm confused. This happens. Loss of meaning. What do they call it? Gestalt collapse.

Everything is weirdly silent. I hear things that are *like* sounds, but I can't believe they're sounds. I can't relate them to me. Why have I entered an unreal world? I might be in danger. I'd better get back. But how? I don't even know where to go back to.

Calm down, Yuki. Take a deep breath. Inhale, exhale. See, your body does what you tell it to. Go ahead, touch it and see—feel your hands and your body. You can feel yourself: you're real. I'm still okay. I'm here. This is my right hand, and this is my left. I can tell them apart.

I try to walk. Where am I? I'll think while I walk.

The atmosphere is heavy and it takes some effort to walk. The air is filled with fine, lead-colored particles. They're soft and warm, and with every step I take they sink into my skin, until they're inside of me. I can feel them covering my skin, and I no longer know where my body leaves off.

Yuck.

With one hand I brush away the particles clinging to my arm. They bounce away like mercury, or like fish scales. But no matter how hard I try, some remain. Gross. The silver specks cover my face and hands. I can't breathe. I'm uncomfortable. I'm buried—I feel as if I'm sinking. I scratch at my face, trying to scrape them off. And when I open my eyes again, my surroundings have changed.

It's like a television screen when the scene shifts. Right, I've changed the channel. So I didn't have to walk at all, all I had to do to get anywhere was to change the channel. But how did I do it? *You idiot, that's not it. You can't change channels. There's only one reality. Your thoughts are faulty. That's it, you're just wrong. There are no particles. It's an illusion. Get a hold of yourself.*

The moment I thought that, the particles vanished.

I breathed easier. I could still think. I'm all right, I

decided.

I was in front of a train station. I could see a little covered shopping arcade. There was a bus stop with several buses lined up at it. Old ticket gates and ticket machines, a realtor, a tobacconist's, a convenience store, a mailbox, a bike rack, a traffic signal, a bookstore. A rusty old bench. I decided to sit down. I needed to try and figure out just what was going on, to gather my wits. I lowered myself onto the bench shakily. Before me people got on buses, got off buses, and walked past like characters in a silent movie. It was too bright out.

I had seen the ghost of an old man. I had smelled death from an old woman's mouth. I had followed them. They had disappeared into a house. Clouds had boiled up like in a time-lapse film. I was surrounded by darkness and couldn't see anything. The next thing I'd known I was in an unfamiliar place. So what had happened? This was no dream. Or, at least, if it was a dream, I'd have to go on living in it. *Think. Grasp the situation.*

Loss of a sense of reality combined with hallucinatory delusions are classic early symptoms of schizophrenia.

Hey, Yuki, that's pretty good. It's amazing you remember that.

Loss of reality comes from a breakdown of the ego. But this couldn't be that. If my ego were shot, I couldn't sit here and think about it. The *me* sitting here thinking was none other than my ego. I wasn't schizophrenic. Yamagishi had said as much. *You're not sick*, he'd said. So I wasn't sick. The confusion I was under was not, could not be, insanity.

Somebody tapped me on the shoulder.

I turned my head and saw a middle-aged woman of about fifty sitting beside me. Her sparse hair was teased up in a perm, exposing her dry scalp. Her face was powdered white and her lips were red, reminding me of those ceremonial masks they used in southeast Asia. When she brought her face close to mine I could smell the powder. "Break down," she said.

I drew back in surprise.

She clutched my arm and repeated, "Break down. Throw it away, everything, break it down." Then she laughed, an unnatural sound that shone in the midday sun.

"What are you saying?"

She wouldn't let go. She was going to tear my arm off. "Throw it away, break it down." Her mouth opened wide like a serpent's.

"Stop it!" Seized with terror, I shook off her grip and started to run.

I kept running into people as I fled. People kept touching my body. Each time I banged into someone, he or she spoke to me, grabbing my arm, pulling my face close to his or hers. *Break down! Break down! Break down!*

Face upon face upon face. Consciousnesses, names, memories. Information about the people I came in contact with invaded my skin as fine silver paticles. The pellets, vibrating slightly, melted into my body. Names: *Akira, Jun, Shoichi,*

Masae, Yoshio, Mari, Nobuhiro, Masayoshi...Watch it! Look where you're going, idiot. Are you okay? What's the matter? Be more careful. Hey, that hurts! Apologize! What's with this bitch—she must be crazy. Thought after thought popped out as particles and permeated me. They were trying to possess me. I didn't want that. Don't come in here. Go away. Don't enter me. I started to shake, like I was tuning in on people's vibrations. Every muscle I had was vibrating independently—I started to cramp up. My body became the dissonance of infinite people. My veins shrank and my breathing became ragged. I'd lost control. There were countless *others* in me.

No. Help. I am disappearing.

Running, I came out into a broad open space. It might have been a park. The place was surrounded by trees whose outstretched branches intertwined in a dark mesh. I saw a jungle gym, a swingset, a slide. In the middle stood a weird *objet d'art* with a dolphin motif. The sculpture's long shadow came directly at me. I ran into the shadow.

I couldn't breathe. I'd run too hard. My heart was ready to leap out of my chest.

I leaned against the statue, gasping, and looked up at the sky.

I heard the distant metallic sound of air currents. Clouds were barreling across the sky. Feeling weak, I crouched down. I gradually lost all sense of my body, until finally all that existed was my heart, beating on. Even then, the *others* continued to vibrate in my cells. Multitudes of people existed in me as palpitations. And they were all murmuring, "Break down."

Break down. Break down. Break down. Break down.

This is an auditory hallucination. Use your head. Think. Thinking is the only thing that can save you now. What's the definition of an auditory hallucination? As though the phrase were the only charm that could restore me to reality, I chant it over and over again: *the definition of an auditory hallucination, the definition of an auditory hallucination, the definition of an auditory hallucination.*

An auditory hallucination is an unconscious emotion or impulse verbalized by the consciousness and projected onto reality.

An auditory hallucination is an unconscious emotion or impulse verbalized by the consciousness and projected onto reality.

An auditory hallucination is an unconscious emotion or impulse verbalized by the consciousness and projected onto reality.

An auditory hallucination is an unconscious emotion or impulse verbalized by the consciousness and projected onto reality.

Way to go, Yuki, woman of reason!

So my own unconscious is telling me to break down. To "throw it away and break it down." Just what am I supposed to throw away? My ego? Don't be silly. If I lose my ego, what happens to me? I'll disappear, won't I? I'll be locked up in a mental hospital to end my days as a derelict. I don't want that. I like this world—I'm pretty happy with it. I'm happy with myself the way I am now. I like *this* Yuki Asakura. I don't want to become a different me.

Suddenly my surroundings went dark. I felt a dull whack against my back. Some viscous substance flowed into me, something that glistened black and ugly like hot tar. It kept flowing into me until it had painted the inside of my head black. I felt pressure and pain behind my nose. Oh, fuck, what now? All sorts of things were pouring into me, incredible qualities in incredible quantities. I was being crushed. This was the void, the vibrations of the omnipresent void. Negative energy.

I bent over and puked up something black and shiny.

A huge amount of tar sprayed onto the ground and melted into the shadow of the statue. It had come to me from the shadow world, that black substance.

I felt a little better after throwing up. But I couldn't stop coughing. Tears of pain welled up.

What's wrong with me? What's happening to me?

I felt as if the surface area of my skin had increased by ten percent. My skin was picking up all kinds of vibrations. I'd become an antenna. My sensory system expanded until I was one huge receptor. I was receiving all of the world's frequencies. I'd lost control. I was like a broken radio.

Somewhere among those myriad frequencies, I sensed my brother.

I missed him so bad. I desperately sought to tune in on

him.

Taka, you fought and struggled all along. I know now. You were in an awful position. I had no idea you were facing this. I can't endure it, everything's coming inside. No wonder you pulled your plug. Teach me how to do it, too. I can't go on like this, I'll go mad.

Somehow, out of a million overlapping frequencies, I managed to pick up my brother's. I was linked to it. I knew I had it, I was sure of it. I'd figured out how to do it. It was so simple—why couldn't I do it until now? All I had to do was sing. Just resonate using the sound inside me. I shouted, and my body became a tube shooting forth sound. My bones quaked. Every cell in my body came alive and started quivering. I was vibrating, subtly and beautifully. And gradually I started to resonate with my brother's vibration. My heart rate rose. I got goose bumps. My teeth chattered. The shaking grew in intensity, and I couldn't stop it. I was becoming something else, transforming into a different vibration. I was scared. I hugged myself and tried to stop shaking, but I couldn't. My consciousness was changing, and I couldn't help it. I was being taken over. This was the end. My cells began to resonate as one with some other thing.

I was turning into something that wasn't me.

Suddenly shards of memory, like fragments of glass, began to rain on me. Large and small, they came tumbling down at me from nowhere and everywhere. Each one of them reflected the memory of a certain point in time and space.

Glinting in the light, the fragments fell into the darkness of my brain.

They were my brother's memories. All of his memories, each one a broken fragment, were being transmitted to my brain. A flood of memories. They'd crush me if I didn't bring them under control. But I didn't know how.

Shiro. The dog, Shiro, being beaten to death. Beaten to death by my dad. Dad, swinging a baseball bat. A sinister reddish-violet mist rises from his body. Dad's soul, drunk, screams in the mist. Saying, *Help me*. Shiro's eye pops out. Taka's face, reflected in that eyeball. Shiro's bloody tail is still wagging, showing affection for Taka. I realize how much my brother had loved Shiro. Taka's memory—Taka's point of view—is one of love. Mom standing over the sink, head down, back turned. A blue mist from her back. The delicate sinews of her neck. The scars on her arms, the slump of her shoulders. Minute recollections of Mom. Mom walking, Mom talking, Mom laughing. Her sadness and bitterness. Dad's face. His drunken, distorted visage, shadows of hatred and terror lurk. Lots of memories of Dad, his hands holding a bowl, his hands beating someone, his mouth yelling, groaning, cursing, belittling, destroying. Fragmented images. When Dad gets angry and jeers, his words give off black soot. Pitch black dust comes pouring out as he speaks. Poisonous words to make you choke. Swallow them and it'll hurt bad. You can't breathe. A gray school like a barracks, children's exposed emotions, all kinds of feelings swirling around in classrooms.

A teacher, suddenly grown into a giant, stands at the lectern and harangues his students. Students rolling their eyes, glass breaking, *don't hit me, don't kick me*, the sour smell of a toilet, the bitter taste of filth, gray particles invading my body, I'm being violated, my mind is being violated. Help. I need a screen. Nobody touch me! Taka thinks. Don't come in. Just leave me alone, please. I'm beginning to fade. I'm beginning to fade. I gave it my all, I really tried to live normally. I wanted to. But I couldn't figure out how. What do I do now? How do I put a stop to this? Everything's pouring into me. I'm resonating with everything. Emotions. The world is made of emotions. I'm going crazy. The only way to stop this invasion is to pull the plug.

The plug was pulled. My brother disappeared.

Suddenly, a blue sky clear as cellophane stretched out before my eyes.

I was free.

I had separated from my body and was now floating, pure consciousness. The world was calm, empty. So quiet.

Had my brother or the schizophrenic boy in the video experienced this freedom?

I wanted to rise up and merge with the blue sky. But I knew that if I did, I'd end up dying like my brother.

The moment I left my body, my memory circuits connected to the world. Now I knew who I was.

Once I'd left the flesh, I was both myself and not myself. I felt profoundly at home, and mysteriously sad.

The wind moaned far away in the vacant sky.

That sound was the beginning of song. The song of the wind resonates with the world. All living things on earth resonate with the wind and produce their own sounds. Once I sang the song of the wind. The sound of air currents, the echoes of the globe—I knew them. So long ago that I couldn't remember when it had been, I had sung the song of the wind for many people, I knew. It had been mine to sing that song over and over.

The wind blows to appease the earth. It's the wind that appeases the earth.

The wind circles the earth, carrying vibrations. The wind produces clouds, causes rain to fall.

Wind and water cause the earth to tremble gently. And that trembling is the source of life.

Now I remember.

The wind blows, clouds rise, and rain falls because that's the prayer of this world.

How could I have forgotten such an important thing for so long?

The next thing I knew, I was sitting on top of the jungle gym.

The sun had set long ago. It was night. Lights burned in houses on the edges of the park. Reddish-black clouds hung in the air above them. The wind blew, pregnant with moisture. Sycamore leaves made a desiccated sound.

Everything was eerily quiet.

Hugging my knees, I gazed at the night sky.

How long had I been there? What was it I'd seen? A dream? A hallucination? No, it had been real. Absolutely real. I knew that, because I could still read the subtle vibrations filling the world. I could still tell that everything, but everything, was shaking.

The atmosphere swayed, full of electricity. I matched my own trembling to it and raised my voice. The air slowly began to resonate with me, whirling, until an updraft appeared and formed rainclouds.

Then silver rain fell from the rainclouds. It fell on my face, my hair, my shoulders. I received the rain with all my heart.

Because the blowing wind, the rainclouds, and the falling rain are the prayer of the world.

The night sky gave off a dull glow, reflecting the lights of Tokyo. From muddy clouds like the belly of a coiled snake I could hear, intermittently, a low moan.

It echoed fear and loathing.

Prayers coexisted with hatred in this world.

I finally understood. The world is a transparency composed of many layers of filters. There are countless phases and their overlapping gives the world its shades.

Each vibration is a filter. If you synchronize with the vibrations you can take them up one by one and observe them.

Some disappear when they overlap. And some manifest themselves. But they all coexist, and they all give shades to the world. The *real* is the sum of all shades.

The universe is composed of vibrations. Life is vibration.

I finally understood everything.

I felt like laughing. All along, it was so simple.

I laughed aloud. I couldn't stop laughing.

Thank you. It's all clear now.

That's enough.

I've got it.

I resonate with all the fine tremblings.

Having sex with the world.

If this is breaking down, it is the ultimate. It's ecstasy.

Want me to throw it all away? Consider it done.

I don't need anything anymore. I'm one with the universe.

I felt constrained by my clothing.

I wanted to take everything off and become nothing but my vibrations.

I took off my shoes and tossed them away. My ring, too. And my watch, and my earrings.

I put my hand in my pocket and found my cell phone.

I was about to toss it away, too, when suddenly I thought of Yamagishi.

He'd implanted a suggestion: *Remember me.* And now it had been triggered.

I looked at the phone, at its green-glowing LCD. I sensed strong electromagnetic interference.

My fingers where they touched the phone felt as if they were burning.

I could perceive the phone circuitry. I could tune myself in on any vibration, instantly. I could even interfere with it.

A connection was made over the line. Probably to Yamagishi.

Yamagishi had foreseen my breakdown. That was why he'd implanted the suggestion.

Remember me.

Thanks. I remembered you.

My last thoughts as the Yuki Asakura you knew were of you.

And then I threw the cell phone into the sky.

22

The first sensation to return to me was sound. A single wave, glowing blue, appeared in the darkness and then vanished. This happened over and over, rhythmically, until finally it became sound.

At first I thought it was music, then realized it was a voice. I didn't understand it, but I recognized a subtle intonation that denoted insecurity.

Next came smell. I detected the mingled odors of blood and disinfectant.

I kept my eyes closed for a while, concentrating on my senses of hearing and smell. Gradually, a visual image took shape in my mind. Strange—I felt as if I were seeing. No, I *was* seeing. With my eyes closed.

My vantage point was a corner of the ceiling. From there, based solely on sound and scent, I could see the room.

Yes. The frequencies, like holographs, carried a wealth of information. The visual image became clearer. A door opened. Footsteps, breathing. All of these were waves. Yamagishi had entered the room. He checked my IV and then peered at my face.

I thought about opening my eyes.

If it wasn't a dream, then when I opened my eyes Yamagishi's face would be right in front of mine.

I decided to give it a shot.

I opened my eyes. There was Yamagishi.

He looked surprised to see my eyelids pop open all of a sudden.

Was this what Yamagishi looked like? I felt as if I were seeing him for the first time. I'd probably never really looked at his face. He had the beginnings of crow's feet around his eyes. The pores on his nose were red. I could clearly see each eyelash, each hair on his cheeks.

"You're awake. How do you feel?"

What a pleasant voice. A nice vibration. I was feeling fine. But I still lacked bodily sensation.

"You're still on medication. You were in quite a state. We pumped you full of sedatives. If we'd let you go on like that your muscles would have given."

I nodded.

"I'm amazed you were able to phone me in your state." Yamagishi touched my fingertips. He loved me. I knew it. Look how much he loved me—that's why he was here. Reality is the answer to every question.

I forced myself to speak. "What happened to me?" My voice was horribly raspy, and my throat hurt.

"You had an acute delusionary episode. You wandered around a residential neighborhood until you finally climbed up onto a jungle gym in a park and stripped off all your clothes. You were yelling that you'd figured out how the universe works, that it's made up of color filters. And then, right in front of the crowd who'd gathered to watch you, you jumped from the top of the jungle gym with absolutely nothing on."

The story was so funny that I couldn't but laugh. When I did, though, my ribs hurt like the devil.

"How did you find me?"

"You called me on your cell phone from the top of the jungle gym. Probably, in the midst of your trance, your ego took emergency measures. I called the cops and told them that one of my patients had escaped. They'd already gotten word of a naked woman making a scene."

It hurt too much to laugh, but I sure wanted to. Instead, I shed tears from the pain.

"Just rest for a while. Don't think about anything," he said, caressing my forehead.

A nurse came to the door and said, "Doctor, your wife is here." Through his fingertips I sensed agitation.

"I'll be back," he said.

As he left, I traced the vibrations he left in his wake. They stayed there for a while, in the air. His vibrations went out into the hall and met up with a different set of vibrations.

They belonged to Ritsuko Honda.

The next day, Ritsuko visited me in my sickroom.

My muscles ached worse than they did the day before. I took the pain as evidence that my head and my body were reconnecting—which was something to be happy about. I felt as if I'd completed a marathon without training for it. All the screws in my body were loose; I could fall apart any minute.

Ritsuko looked very concerned.

"I'm okay," I told her. I knew she was worried about my future.

She wondered if I'd continue having such episodes. Would I be able to lead a normal life? Once you've collapsed, it's hard not to let it happen again. It becomes a habit. I was calm now, but how long would that last? Maybe I really was crazy. Maybe my personality was disintegrating.

Those worries weren't like Ritsuko. I couldn't believe that she still clung to such concepts as "a normal life." Everything struck me as hilarious.

"It's all right, I won't break down again. And I won't die, either, so relax."

She gave me a suspicious, questioning look.

Oh, right, she hadn't said anything. "Your friend died, right?"

All expression vanished from her face.

"Your friend, the reason you started researching shaman-ism. The one who went nuts like me and had to be committed. She killed herself, didn't she? Just before you went to Okinawa."

"How do you know that?"

Her body radiated fear, which looked like red powder.

"You told me yourself that the world has a host computer where all memory is stored, and if you access it, you can call up any memory you like. If I do a search based on your vibrations, I can pull up your memories of her. The universe is organized and classified by frequency. Everything is converted to data by means of vibrations—consciousness and physicality both."

She was visibly shaken. She'd said much the same, but she'd never believed it.

"Are you telling me that you've accessed the host?"

I shook my head. "It seems I've been connected to it all along—I was born that way."

I felt her weak but definite denial; she was resisting the idea.

"Your friend was genuinely grateful to you, Ritsuko. You were the only person who really tried to understand her. She knew that. She wasn't crazy. All she did was put out her antenna; but when she did, she started receiving all sorts of interference and she got confused. Just like me. She wasn't mentally ill. There were things she had to do, and she was prevented from doing them, all because they thought she was sick…"

"When did you find out all that?"

Find out? I just *knew* it. "Probably when you told me about her. I think I already knew at that time, I just wasn't conscious of it. The information was still locked in my subconscious."

"Sorry, I'm having a little trouble understanding all this. What proof can you give me that you're telling the truth?"

So it was proof she wanted. "You said the play the two of you had gone to see was Soh Kitamura's *Hymn*. But actually, it was *Hymn 2*, wasn't it?"

What I felt from her now was less surprise than envy. It seemed she hadn't been interested in researching shamanism so much as in becoming a shamaness herself. She had her heart set on it. That's why she'd taken an interest in me.

"It was the medication that killed your friend. They gave her lots of drugs to calm her down, and it made her groggy. She wasn't sick—there was no need to dull her mind like that. I think it was really tough on her. Her body felt like lead. And in that drug-induced haze, she tuned into a certain strong wavelength and synchronized with it. We—she and I—are outlets, who can pull energy out of our unconscious with no loss of ego. The ego plays a very important role for us. And in her case, her ego had been weakened by medication. So she allowed herself to be influenced by negative interference. Like the curses the vengeful dead leave on places they hated. She started to resonate with one of those bad vibes."

Ritsuko was crying. I'd never seen her cry. "You're right. She was on a trip, and in her hotel room one night she slit her wrists."

There's no need to cry, Ritsuko. Your gut feeling was right, and her death wasn't your fault. It was an accident.

"But me, I'm all right. Thanks to Yamagishi, I don't seem to be here as a mental patient. They're not giving me medication. Once I get my strength back I think I ought to be able to make a go of it. Don't worry about me."

Ritsuko stared at me. "You seem different, Yuki."

"You think so? I can't tell myself."

"You've changed. You're like a different person."

Why was she weeping so much? "Oh, and it turns out Yamagishi's married to *you*."

Her reactions were always so easy to interpret. Her earlobes suddenly went scarlet. "How did you know? Did he tell you?"

"No. I just sort of got it."

She sighed. "I didn't start out intending to hide that from you. I mean, the subject of marriage just hadn't come up—there wasn't any reason for me to tell you I was married—before you unexpectedly mentioned Mineo. And then when you did, I somehow couldn't tell you the truth. Maybe I was jealous because I knew he'd had a crush on you in college. And I didn't want him to get involved with you—you seemed as wild and dangerous as ever. To be frank, I don't like women like you. I didn't want you near me and I certainly didn't want to get into a contest with you over a man. There was no way I could win. And yet, I, like Mineo, couldn't resist you. For different reasons, of course."

I felt sorry for Ritsuko. She was always seeking something she didn't have. She'd married Yamagishi for the same reason she'd been drawn to me. But whatever you seek eludes you the more you pursue it.

"You know, Yuki, Mineo loves you."

"So?"

"So I'm angry. I want to kill you." She gave a self-deprecating laugh.

Once I checked out of the hospital, I'd probably go out of

their lives forever. I had to. The thought didn't upset me. I said, "I'm thinking of going to Okinawa as soon as I get out of this place."

"Okinawa? To see a *yuta*?"

Exactly. I had to get one to teach me about myself. I didn't understand the first thing about the way I was. What should I do, how should I live? What was I? Okinawa seemed to offer some answers.

It struck me as funny, though—maybe I hadn't changed a bit. I hadn't known what I was before, either. I hadn't known what to do, how to live. Maybe I'd always be a riddle to myself. Maybe there *was* no "me" squatting in my body, maybe I was just something formed of various strains of interference, maybe I was something that would go on changing forever. If that was the case, there was no point in "selfhood." It was meaningless. But the meaninglessness was the whole point. Man, what had taken me so long?

As I chuckled to myself, Ritsuko looked at me with fear in her eyes. *Don't look at me like that. This is me, the new me, the original me.*

"By the way, Kunisada called," she said. "He's worried about you. He said he keeps calling you but there's no answer, and do I know what's up. I lied and told him you'd gone back to your parents' house. I mean, there was no way I could explain to him everything that's happened."

"Thanks. You did the right thing."

I'd almost forgotten. There was someone else I had to say goodbye to. A very special goodbye.

"So how are you feeling today?"

We hadn't seen each other for a month, but still Kunisada was saying the same old thing. Disgusted, I sat down in front of him and crossed my legs. "I'm doing wonderfully, Professor."

"Well, that's good. I hear you've been sick this last month. I take it you're fully recovered?"

"Yes. Body and mind."

"Excellent, excellent." He studied me carefully. Maybe his professional interest had helped him detect the change in me.

"And so, Professor, although this is kind of sudden, I'd like to make today our last session."

For a moment he looked crushed. He heaved a sigh, scratched his head, and said, "Why?"

"There's no need to continue."

"And why is that?"

"Everything has changed," I said crisply, in a way I could tell made him anxious.

He shifted in his chair and requested, his voice heavy: "Would you mind being more specific?"

What could I tell him, specifically? I doubted there was anything I could say that his brain could comprehend. "Hmm. How about if *I* asked *you* something for a change?"

"All right. Ask, then." He leaned forward.

Chuckling, I asked, "When you stuck your penis into my outlet, Professor, what were you accessing?"

Tremors contorted his features. "What are you talking

about? I don't understand the meaning of your question."

"I'm asking, what were you accessing when we had sex, when you inserted your penis into my vagina? You were accessing something, no? My body is an outlet. Stick in a plug and all sorts of things come flowing out."

"Ms. Asakura. When did you start to think of things in these terms? Is this something you came up with on your own? Or did somebody else put it in your head?" His eyes were turning crimson.

"Oh, Professor, of course it's just my very own delusion. My consciousness is verbalizing data from my unconscious. It's just a delusion. Anything and everything exists in the unconscious, doesn't it, Professor? It's a cornucopia with everything in it—primitive instincts, violent impulses, repressed lusts, collective memories. So why shouldn't there be a great deal of truth stuffed in there, too? And I figured it out: if the ego could keep functioning normally while verbalizing, visualizing, vocalizing data from the unconscious, then a person could do anything. I don't know the proper method of conversion yet, that's all. The unconscious is actually a terminal, connected to a host computer somewhere. I don't know how I access it. I have no manual. But even so, you shouldn't scoff at my delusions, Professor. Delusions don't belong solely to mental patients, you know. I say it's time to bring our delusions out of the shadows, Professor Kunisada."

"What's happened to you, Ms. Asakura? You're acting strangely today."

"Is it not your job to deal with the strange?" I had a good

long laugh. Fear began to show on his face. I stood up slowly and said, "Don't be afraid, Professor."

"I'm not afraid. I'm simply taken aback."

"Now, remember, Professor. Remember sex with me. It was good, wasn't it? What did you feel? Can you remember it? Or do you need to plug in one more time?"

I could tell he was having flashbacks. I tried to read them, but couldn't convert them into visual information. But I was able to get general impressions: sweet mounds of flesh, soft white flesh.

A-ha. His mother. When he was having sex with me, he was making love to his mother.

"I see, Professor—you have an Oedipal complex. When you were licking my nipples you were actually sucking at your mother's breast. No wonder you felt so guilty about sex that you had to masturbate and come alone, outside of me."

In Freudian terms, he'd suffered a libidinal disturbance during the oral stage.

"What…what are you saying? Show some respect. What's wrong with you?"

"It's just a delusion, Professor. What are you getting so angry about?"

"Are you trying to provoke me?" He sounded on the verge of tears.

"When I abandoned you, Professor, it was as if your mother were abandoning you all over again. Your mother died young, didn't she? You still harbor resentment over that."

"Yuki, that's enough!"

"My delusions aren't that far off the mark, are they, Professor?" I hiked up my skirt and slowly stripped off my panties. "If you're not quiet, Professor, somebody'll find us out. Don't you want to say a proper goodbye?"

I walked over to him and held his head to my breasts. He was sobbing like a baby. I unzipped his trousers; his penis was already hard. I coaxed it out of the flap in his briefs and then lowered myself on top of it. I could feel it twitch and pulse.

"Do you want to lick my breasts?"

He nodded furiously. I lifted my bra and let him suck on my nipples. He sucked for all he was worth, moving his hips all the while. If I let myself go, let myself respond to a man, I could draw forth the sweet feelings of his pleasure.

It's utterly amazing what debauched fantasies people can excite themselves with.

Right. Sensitivity is the ultimate sensuality.

He receded further and further into infantile memories of being clutched to his mother's breast. Replaying these memories of love drew huge amounts of life energy from the surrounding atmosphere, and these were poured into the man's spirit until he was filled with energy. Enough to wash away hatred, sorrow, and pain.

This was true healing.

I couldn't but laugh, out of joy. Every day was a new discovery.

"Professor, I'm grateful to you. If I hadn't met you, I'd never have awakened to sex. If I'd never known sensuality I'd never have been able to attain sensitivity. I'm sure you have no idea what I'm talking about, though."

Before long he climaxed, ejaculating inside me.

"Aw, what a bad boy. If I have a baby, I'm gonna send it to you. Raise it well, okay?"

Spent, he nodded faintly. In his ecstasy he looked like an infant. I used his necktie to wipe the semen off my genitals. Then I put on my panties and fixed on my clothes.

"Well, then, Professor. This time it's really goodbye."

I turned him around in his swivel chair so he was facing the blinds. It wouldn't do to have anybody come in and find him with his penis hanging out.

The door banged shut behind me.

My body still tingled—it wanted more pleasure. I was consuming a kind of energy you can't get from food. I was imbibing energy by responding to another person. It was actually decreasing my food intake.

Sex, the ultimate diet.

I laughed again. I felt triumphant. I'd never in my life felt so fulfilled, so *good*. Everything was brand new. I was high. I could feel energy passing straight through my body and into the ground. Everything that had been impeding the flow was now gone.

23

The Fasten Seatbelts sign went off.

The plane must have entered its flight path for Okinawa. I unfastened my seat belt and took out a manila envelope from the bag at my feet. Inside it was a document of a dozen or more photocopied pages.

The cover read, *The Life of a Yuta, Miyo Kamichi: An Oral History*. Ritsuko had sent it to me by express delivery the day before. Ritsuko's vibrations lingered faintly on the pages, like fond memories from decades ago.

I turned the page and was confronted by blocks of dense type. I turned on the light and started to follow the tribulation-filled life of Miyo Kamichi, shamaness.

Physical ailments. Migraines. Removal of her uterus due to a myoma. A succession of family catastrophes, marriage and divorce, a fire at her home which almost killed her and left her with terrible burns. The sudden death of her son. This woman was like a catalog of misfortune.

At the end of the report, Ritsuko had appended a note.

After the death of her son, the subject experienced an intense trance episode called "kamidari." A relative took her to see another relative who was a yuta. Through "yutagutu" [yuta rituals], the subject

was recognized as a "kaminchu" [one who is to become a yuta]. The
subject spent seven difficult years searching before finally construct-
ing her own spiritual system. Finally she met her "chiji" [tutelary
deity]. Since that point, the chiji [in her case, a white dragon god]
has been her possession-personality.

What was a possession-personality? Maybe it acted as a
sort of modem when she accessed the host? Maybe she verbalized the information she took from the unconscious by
projecting it onto the possession-personality. Or maybe there
really were gods. If so, I wanted to meet them. Whatever they
were.

Miyako Island has vibrations quite different from the
main islands of Japan. The vibrations are stronger, and they
come welling up out of the ground as if the earth itself is resonating. The minute I got off the plane I felt the ground move
beneath me. Those vibrations are what make Okinawa so
unique. I was sure that the *yuta* must be those who were sensitive to the vibrations of this land.

All I had to do was tell the taxi driver Miyo Kamichi's
name and address. Fifteen minutes later, I was standing in
front of her house. The house stood alone near a cluster of sea-
side dwellings. In front of it stood huge ficus trees, dangling
their aerial roots.

A ceramic lion gazed down at me from the roof. The air
smelled of fruit and animals.

I called out and was immediately answered. The front door slid open.

A middle-aged woman who looked like a maid stepped out.

"I've come from Tokyo," I said. "Ritsuko Honda arranged a visit for me."

The lady grinned and said, "Come right in."

I entered to find myself in a small dirt-floored area. In the room beyond it was a strange altar. It was surrounded by so many sake bottles and soft drink containers and so much fruit that there was almost no place to stand.

In front of the altar sat a plump woman. Her frame was small, but somehow she gave an impression of great mass. *Tiny but dense*, was what I thought.

And that mass influenced the air around her. It was as if her density had created its own magnetic field.

"I was told that a strong light would be coming from the East. I was waiting for you," she said, and flashed a friendly smile.

I bowed silently.

She urged me to take a seat beside her, so I took off my shoes and stepped in.

There was no small talk. She started right in with the ceremony. She took a deep breath, opening her mouth wide, and then flipped her switch.

I could tell that she was trying to tune herself in to a frequency. What frequency? I decided to try to tune in to it myself.

But the moment I tried to sensitize myself, I felt my blood begin to boil. I gave up, alarmed.

I felt as if my heart would stop. This was new to me. I couldn't synchronize with this vibration. Maybe it was a frequency of blood—maybe only people who shared the same blood could tune in.

Beating time on her left knee, Miyo began to chant.

The chant must have been in the Okinawan dialect—I couldn't understand a word. But from the sounds she was making I was somehow able to grasp the meaning.

She was calling to somebody.

She was summoning something like the spirit of the earth, sleeping deep in the ground.

Soil, water, magma, the dead—it was a song meant to resonate with the vibrations of the rulers of the underworld.

And I heard an echo from the ground. The same thing I'd felt at the airport.

It passed through Miyo. She was receiving the ground-frequency and using her mass to convert it.

She'd already lost consciousness—she was in a trance state. I wondered why she went to the trouble of entering a trance. Losing consciousness put her at risk, didn't it?

A-ha, I got it. Her ego wouldn't survive the conversion process—that's why she relied on the possession-personality to convert the vibrations. It enabled her to convert some terrific earth-energy and to send it flowing into people's plugs.

In which case, her god was nothing more than a frequency-converting tool.

Miyo converted the earth-vibrations and sent them into me.

I could receive them now. They were at a different voltage than before.

My cells, one by one, altered their vibrations—my insides started to change.

But it was okay. I could watch my transformation, feel it, as myself.

Time to manifest yourself, Okinawan gods. What do you have to show me?

What I saw was my brother's corpse.

Which I'd never actually seen. It was lying on the kitchen tiles in that apartment.

He was still newly dead, and hadn't yet begun to turn pale. He looked alive, in fact. He was still emitting a life energy in faint amounts. Then, as if fast-forwarding through a video, I saw his corpse stiffen. Once in a while a joint would twitch as part of the natural process of rigor mortis. His skin changed color. Blood began to flow from every opening, and his flesh turned greenish-yellow. Rot set in.

Microbes bred in his mouth, and maggots started to

emerge. My brother's body became a host for microorganisms, and they hastened his decomposition. His flesh was quickly broken down until it could no longer retain its shape; it collapsed, it wore away.

Finally, only his bones were left.

His flesh had returned to the earth, where it was further broken down by bacteria, becoming nutrients, leaching into the groundwater, flowing into swamps, into rivers, into the sea, evaporating and rising into the sky to become clouds, and finally raining onto the earth like mercy.

Rain, rain, rain. Pouring rain. Purifying rain. I received it on my upturned face.

The wind blows, clouds form, and rain falls because that's the prayer of this world.

Miyo's song was over.

She looked me in the eye and asked, "Do you see? We appease the spirits."

I lowered my head.

For a long time I had wanted to know what prayer was. And now I knew. I bowed deeply before Miyo, deeper than I'd ever bowed to anyone before in my life. I couldn't bow deeply enough, I felt. I never knew gratitude could bring such pleasure. How long had I been unable to feel genuine gratitude? How long had my ego been infantile?

"I have nothing to teach you. You are a new life. You have

something we do not have. If we are the priestesses of ancient nature, you might be a budding priestess of the new earth. Just as you suspected, we *yuta* do our work through divine possession. That is how we have been taught to do it since ancient times. For thousands of years we have connected to the gods thus. But today, there are fewer and fewer people willing to accept it when a *yuta* becomes possessed and starts acting wildly. Even here in Okinawa, there are some who feel our very existence is undesirable. They even have their own, new religions, it seems. Alas, we know no way to connect to the gods other than to be possessed by them. You seem to know another way, and what is more, you were born that way. I imagine more and more people like you will be born in the years to come. New priestesses, born of a new nature. Several thousand years have passed since the first prayer, and the earth has changed. It's only natural that priestesses should change, too. And so I have nothing to teach you. You should carry out your own work in your own way, and that will be enough. Just now I showed you a spirit-appeasing prayer. That's all I can do for you."

I raised my head and asked, "So what should I do?"

Miyo cackled. "Even if I knew, I wouldn't tell you."

Now I had to laugh. She was right, of course.

"It seems," she said, "that your late brother was guiding you."

"Guiding me?"

"He left powerful thoughts on this earth in order to tell you something, to give you the chance to transform yourself.

Why don't you release him?"

I had to translate her words into language I could understand. She seemed to be saying that my brother transferred lots of vibrations to this world when he died in order to help me grow. Which meant that it must have been my sensitivity to those vibrations that had caused me to see him. And now she was telling me to release those vibrations.

Release the vibrations. Appease the dead.

"How do I do that? Is it something I can do?"

She nodded forcefully.

"Remember what I tell you. What's important is the place. Find the right place and go there. If a person is in the right place, she'll always do the right thing."

24

The predawn air was cold.

But it had to be, it was late November. I could see my breath when I exhaled.

I was standing on a road between dark fields, staring at an unmanned railroad crossing lit by a mercury lamp.

If I was going to meet my brother, this had to be the place. This was where I'd first seen him.

Five in the morning. Dawn was just around the corner. The plants were waking up, starting to breathe. I could sense the atmosphere's oxygen content rising. The air was thick.

As the plants awoke, so did moving things. I could sense birds and insects.

I myself wasn't sure why I'd chosen this particular time. I just knew it had to be right before dawn. The moments between night and morning, that zone, had to be the best time for liberating trapped vibrations.

I took a deep breath, and then extended my right hand toward the heavens.

I thought this would enable me to feel it more easily. I was going on intuition, since I had no manual.

I concentrated on my right hand and searched for Taka's

vibration, cautiously and slowly. Grasses, trees, microorganisms, insects, minerals, water—all these vibrations together made up dawn. And among them, I searched for where my brother's might be hiding.

There he was.

I opened my eyes, and Taka was standing on the other side of the tracks.

My mind was no longer bound by the idea that my brother was in fact my brother. My brother both was my brother and wasn't my brother—that was how things stood. Peeled clean of everything human, only the essence of my brother remained: a sad, kind spirit.

"I finally made it," I said—but silently, inwardly. "Thanks to you. I'm grateful."

I altered the frequency of my cells and tried to match his wavelength. When I succeeded, my brother's thoughts came from the image projected on the other side of the tracks.

We were brother and sister, and shared the same gift, but it was all we could do to protect our own egos, you yours and me mine. So we never got to resonate with each other. Too bad, don't you think?

We lived in fear, all of us, resenting our own innocence and the arrogance of the rest of the world. We lived inside shells, to keep from being overwhelmed by the world. If we let our guards down even for a minute, we got swamped by those terribly powerful interferences called human emotions. They'd invade us, and destroy us. Take over our egos. We were misunderstood, and life was hard. But that's over now.

Thanks to you, I've been able to gain a new consciousness.

I've cast off my shell, too.

Thank you.

The sky was growing pale with the dawn.

I sang a prayer-song.

Where had I learned it? It was less a song than pure sound.

A sound like the wind soughing.

A lullaby sung by the earth as it turned.

The wind appeases the earth.

The wind blows through the world, forms clouds, and causes rain to fall.

And it appeases the earth.

The sound and my brother's lingering vibration resonated.

They turned into harmonizing vibrations and rose up.

And then, sucked heavenward, they were gone.

I felt warm light on my cheeks. Sunrise.

The edges of the mountains surrounding the valley were on fire.

Orange sunlight from an ultramarine sky. The warmed air started to rise from the fields, taking moisture with it.

The smell of countless creatures living in the earth. More: scents of living things arose from houses, from concrete, from rivers and sewers. The fresh smell of life rejoicing in the dawn. I almost gagged on it.

Every living thing gave off a scent, and the universe resonated with those odors.

Standing there in the soft light, I inhaled as much of the ozone-filled air as I could. As I exhaled it I savored the smell, a fresh, raw smell.

Wait.

I smelled my brother in the air. The scent of his rotting flesh.

I concentrated on that smell, trying to isolate the odor of death, but to my surprise I found that it was part of *all* the smells. It was composed of particles so small that they couldn't be broken down any further—*and they were evenly distributed among the smells of all living things.*

It wasn't a bad smell at all.

25

I'm living in Shibuya now, the part of Tokyo I'd once hated so much.

I'm here because there are a lot of people here who are like my brother, like the old me. People living in shells to protect themselves. Afraid they'll be overrun if they don't.

I've taken to calling us all—myself, my brother, and the rest of us—Outlets.

To an Outlet, parents and siblings are invaders. People close to us are dangerous, because we'll respond to their emotions. Outlets live their lives at the mercy of others' emotions.

It's nobody's fault. We're just born with a special sensitivity, that's all. At bottom, an Outlet is a shaman with the power to respond to a rare and different world.

Outlets with weak egos are taken to be mad. Outlets like me, with somewhat stronger egos, manage to muddle through. In either case, we have to struggle to adapt to society. We're treated as freaks.

If an Outlet goes on blocking out other people's emotions for long enough, he or she will start to hate humanity. Outlets with their blinds shut seem to outsiders to be concerned only with themselves and the passing moment.

Outlets, by their nature, have a tendency to slip into trancelike states, or to snap. We're dangerous people. Hard to understand. But an awakened Outlet has the power to heal people's traumas in the blink of an eye.

There are a lot of us scattered around the city. When I meet them, I teach them about vibrations, about breakdowns, and about how to resonate.

I put up a homepage on the internet and posted my experiences. A great many Outlets accessed them.

The biggest problem is when the time comes to break down.

You don't lose yourself when you break down. It's all right. You break down in order to change. That's how the OS of your consciousness works. The essence of your soul doesn't change. An Outlet's ego doesn't have many desires to begin with. Any desires an Outlet does have tend to be responses to others' desires. So Outlets break down easily. You don't have to retreat to a mountain and undergo great austerities—you can do it here and now. For an Outlet, having a breakdown is a form of self-realization.

Of course, even when I put it like that, as positively as I can, you'll be afraid. But no matter how scared you are, you'll break down when the time comes, so be prepared. Only you know when it'll happen to you.

If and when a breakdown comes suddenly, it's much better to know what's going on as it dredges up past traumas. Understanding that is far preferable to ending up in an asylum.

I'd typed that much when the doorbell rang. I had company, it seemed.

"Coming," I said, walking away from the computer. I kept the chain on and opened the door just wide enough to check the caller's letter of introduction. Then I undid the chain and let him in.

Most of the men who come here are white-collar workers in their twenties or thirties. Sometimes I get older men, but I don't have much use for them. Time's limited, and the future won't be helped much by my healing middle-aged men.

Today it was a thirty-three-year-old office worker. He looked utterly worn-out. I showed him into the room I called my Counseling Room.

There wasn't much in the room. White blinds on the window, a sofa, and a plain, simple bed.

He looked uncomfortable as he sat down on the sofa. It was his first time, and he seemed nervous.

"It's all right," I laughed.

"It's just that I've never been to a place like this before…" He wiped his sweaty face with a handkerchief. "Are you sure ten thousand yen is enough?"

I lowered the blinds and then approached him. I loosened his tie for him.

"Don't worry about the money. I basically consider this volunteer work anyway."

His nose was twitching. "Wh-why do you do this?"

As I stripped off his clothes, I couldn't help but be struck by how funny it all was. "Why do I do it? As long as I can remember, I've felt duty-bound to sleep with as many men as possible. Think about it. The world's been changed by vaginas. It was *this* that gave courage to men on battlefields. It was *this* that took in untold numbers of invaders and brought forth new bloodlines, integrating the whole world. It's the world's power outlet."

I get that question a lot. When I undid his trousers, his penis was still soft. That was because he asked stupid questions.

"But aren't you...miserable?"

He sounded at his wits' end. What a strange man. I glanced at his face. With his sad, lost expression he looked like the young Dustin Hoffman acting his heart out. I felt I'd seen his face somewhere before. When had it been? I had only hazy memories of my pre-breakdown days.

"Why should I be miserable? An Outlet lives by responding. What she responds to is up to her; in my case, it's pretty straightforward."

I took his penis into my mouth and gently worked it with my tongue. I could feel it growing inside me, starting to tremble. That's it, tremble. Tremble with your very own vibrations. That's what will bring out your power to live. Remember your own life-vibrations.

What sensations were about to be awakened in him? Just thinking about it made me wet.

There you go. Plug in.